Three Men in a Tub

By

Randy R. Pischel

ISBN-10 :0615893511

ISBN-13 :9780615893518

First Edition Paperback

For
Edith

1

Scotty Rutherford had a habit of coming home late and falling on his stomach fully dressed with his feet hanging over the side of the bed. It was comfortable and he'd doze off for a few moments before pulling himself together enough to continue his night of eating pizzas and watching the tube. He never once thought that this would lead to his death.

On this particular night a thin red line, one that would have made any physicist on Earth drool in amazement, snaked down from the ceiling and neatly wrapped itself around the dangling leg that hung loosely over the edge of the bed. It was a very easy target.

Once firmly attached to his ankle the red line lifted Scotty up off the bed, waking him very abruptly from his muddled dreams. In his last few seconds of life many thoughts crossed his mind but none would firmly take hold.

The light slid effortlessly through the ceiling but his foot rather clumsily punched through the drywall and pink insulation beyond. Unfortunately for Scotty the studs that held the drywall in place were rather heavy and did not give way when a split second later his hip crashed into one. However the light was relentless and kept its upward path through the roof and up into the sky but rather than an entire Scotty Rutherford it merely had his foot, and parts of his calf, and a few unidentifiable dangly things. The rest of Scotty crashed back down into the bedroom, flipped off the side of his bed, and lay on the floor panting.

He was so shocked and surprised at this unexpected event that he bled to death before he even realized his foot had gone missing.

A few moments later the missing foot in question dropped out of the sky, bounced off his roof, and nearly hit his grill when it landed in the back yard.

Later that week when a worried coworker reported his body to the police they could only come to the conclusion that his death was "suspicious."

Exactly 1127 miles and three days away Nathan Mann did not fare much better. For although the owners of the red line had researched the proper function of the red line and had thought they had figured it out poor Nathan was left armless and lifeless after the red line tried to pull him out of the ceiling of his second story loft located in a four story building. The results were much worse and police in this case had no words to put on their reports to say how stumped they were for an explanation.

The owners of the red line thought they had everything figured out yet again when they lowered it towards Arnold Raushen.   Arms and legs were weak, they reckoned, they should attach the red line to a much thicker part of the anatomy. The thicker part they chose however was also used for breathing and swallowing and for sending blood to the brain and stopping these functions turned out to be just as bad as yanking him from his favorite spot on the couch through the ceiling.

After a few more unsuccessful attempts to use the red line the owners sent it hurtling into deep space along with its owner manual, which was written by the lowest bidder. They decided to use a more old-fashioned hands-on approach which involved less physics and was much more likely to yield a healthy, living adult male.

***

Joel looked up at the starry sky, what he could see of it, and took a deep breath. The air smelled like greasy hamburgers and French fries and was filled with the sound of chatter. The retro Burger Bar was always busy and they only hired the best looking women on campus.

"Joel, you got the tickets, right?"

"Yes, and I got double the bacon, right?"

The girl's name was Patty and she was gorgeous and Joel spent a good chunk of his student loan trying to impress her. Surprisingly it was an Abba tribute band that made the difference and he thought he was finally going to cross the bridge from hanging out with her to actually dating her. It felt kind of anti-climactic to him, though, as another girl had caught his eye some days before and he was already using his moves on her.

He flirted until she absolutely had to get back to work then went back to his convertible Chevy. It was a 70's tank and well known around campus as Joel always liked being where the action was. He sat for a moment and couldn't believe the beautiful girls that were hanging out tonight.

Life was good.

He looked back up at the stars. He wanted to see more of them. Getting out of the city seemed like a good idea and half an hour later he was officially out of town and enjoying the clear country air. He wanted to find a nice place to pull over, enjoy his bacon burger and shake, and just stare at the stars.

The trees grew thicker here and the corn fields filled in the rest of the vista but at night it all blended together anyway. He passed several cars, a reminder that he was still near the city. Another reminder was the dull yellow glow on the horizon in his rear-view mirror. He just had to find some solitude somewhere. A dirt road was needed, something with no traffic and maybe a little trail he could pull off on.

He only vaguely thought about the studying he should be doing as he gunned the engine once more. And he never even gave a second thought to the headlights that shone distantly in his rear-view mirror.

At least not until he realized how fast they were gaining on him.

The lights filled up his rear-view mirror hurting his eyes. He slowed down and moved towards the right side of the road but the lights persisted. He squinted and could see not two but five lights in his mirror. He flicked it towards the floor and moved as far as he could to the right and when the lights continued to ride his tail he did his last resort move.

He slammed on the brakes.

Unfortunately this made his car stall. There wasn't another sound. He threw his arm over the seat to see what he was facing and wondered what he could use as a weapon should this turn into a road rage issue. Dust slowly settled around his car as he glared at the lights.

Then, very silently they floated up over his car.

The realization came on slowly. He watched as whatever it was slowed and stopped, with the white, headlamp-looking lights still shining down at him. Then it hit him.

He was scared shitless. There was just no other way of describing it. He was absolutely petrified. Whatever it was, it was slowly floating over his car. He tried to reach the ignition but his hand just sort of waved in the direction of the steering column, his eyes glued on the lights. The thought that this is what deer must feel like almost made him laugh. How absurd that he was so scared and this stupid thought should enter his head. At least it woke him up.

Coming to his senses and fighting panic, he managed to turn the key. He wished that just for this moment he had the top up so he would feel at least a little bit safe but it wasn't, and he felt quite naked. The lights were slowly advancing up over his car lighting his interior with a blinding white light. Why, he thought, wouldn't his car start?

It was directly over him now.

He looked up at the smooth metal underside of whatever it was and saw that it was circular and surrounded with the little white lights. A circle. A flying saucer. By god, it looked just like those photographs that everybody fakes. A smooth flying disk with lights around it.

The last thing he remembered was how silly and embarrassed he would be if he actually tried to tell anybody about this.

2

Matt plopped down in his favorite chair, aching from the day's work. But it was a good ache, he thought. He actually got a lot done, a lot of little things that had been nagging him around the farm. He serviced two of the tractors and one of the trucks, fixed the fences on the west range, and still managed to find time to shoot some cans down by the dump and do the rest of his regular chores. He opened up the west range from Cutter's range and let the cows roam free. The grass had grown so long from it being closed all summer that the cows would feast tonight.

He looked at his big, callused hands, still dark with grease and oil after his shower, and wondered what Melody saw in him. He was, after all, just his father's farm hand and at 30, still didn't live on his own yet. His father did give him an acre off the county road a few years back but he never had the money to build on it. Now that he was engaged and time was pressing he would probably just put a trailer on it. He had looked at some weeks earlier and they really weren't that bad. Well, Melody liked them anyway, and that's all that really mattered.

He pushed back in the chair and the foot rest shot out, hanging down on one side from years of wear. Even though it was late he thumbed through the TV Guide to see if there was anything worth watching, but there didn't seem to be.

On a whim he picked up the phone and dialed Melody's number. It rang three times, two more than she ever let it, so he hung up. She was probably at her mother's or sister's so had her phone muted. He wondered how her diet was going and if she'd ever fit into the dress she bought and if they'd ever really set a date for her to wear it.

But that didn't matter to him. He was in love with her and that's what did matter.

Just then the phone rang, bringing him abruptly out of the light snooze he had fallen into.

"Oh, crap." He said. "Where at? Well, I'll be there in about half an hour."

He walked to the stairs and yelled up, "Dad, hey dad. I'm gonna need your help."

An old, scratchy voice answered him, "What is it?" Matt's father came slowly down the stairs, his years readily seen in his face. "What is it?" He said again.

"I let the cows in the west range today. But apparently they got out."

"Ya fixed the fence, didn't ya?"

"Of course I fixed the fence. They're on Surrey road, so there must be a new break along that side. The sheriff is there now."

"Well, let's go." His father was well accustomed to taking care of these things and never wasted time wondering or talking about how things came about. "You take the tractor and go along the fence. I'll go over to Rogers place and round up his kids. They'll love chasing cows at night."

Matt smiled at the thought of his brother's kids rounding up the loose cows. It wasn't the first time and he knew it wouldn't be the last. As he headed towards the tractor he wondered if his kids would be roused out of bed to help their grandfather someday.

The tractor lumbered out of the yard and down the short hill to the gate. He would have to check the fence from the inside to avoid the ditches and trenches. The spotlight shone brightly in the dark night and cast eerie shadows in the grasses and on the hills.

He wasn't far from the gates when he noticed lights coming from the other direction along the fence. Who on earth could it be? The night must have been playing tricks on his eyes because he couldn't tell which side of the fence they were on. It almost seemed that they were straddling the fence.

Or floating above it.

Matt stopped the tractor and rubbed his eyes. Sure enough, it seemed to be floating above the fence. He couldn't see past the lights but the lights themselves were in a circle.

He sat there, transfixed, absolutely not knowing what to do. In the end he decided to just watch it. He had the thought to shut off the tractor to see if he could hear anything, but all he was met with was an eerie silence. He slowly turned the spot towards it but it was far out shone by the lights staring back at him.

The thing kept floating towards him and still he was more curious than scared.

This was the coolest thing, by far, that he had ever seen. And with that thought he passed into unconsciousness.

3

Gary checked his watch but it didn't even register what time it was. It was more a habit than anything else. A thought struck him and he checked it again, now getting the time. He had two more miles to go and plenty of time to shower and still get home in time to see the match. Soccer was his favorite sport but it was always on at funny hours and almost never live. Good thing he was considering a job offer in South America. Then he could attend matches in person.

He jogged on taking in the scenery. The mountains never ceased to amaze him having grown up in the Great Plains. Sometimes he felt sorry for the people who grew up here, they never seem to appreciate what they have and he was surprised at how many locals couldn't even name the mountains around them.

Sweat rolled in his eyes and despite the breeze he could smell various odors rising up from his body. Yes, today he definitely needed that shower.

As he approached the city he went over his mental checklist. Take the rest of the night off, breakfast early, meet with his boss at eight, and go over the proposal to start a factory in Brazil. Not that it would be huge or anything, but he would head up the project and that meant a good-sized raise and some solid footing in the company. Who would've thought rubber parts for cell phones would become big business?

The city popped up suddenly around him. He slowed to a walk to cool down and even though he was dripping with sweat he decided to get some magazines in case the soccer match was preempted by skateboarding or some other stupid thing. The female clerk smiled as he passed his Scientific American, Discover, and PC Digest over the counter but he missed it. Even though he was told time and time again how good looking he was, he never seriously believed it. He just liked to keep fit, keep working, and keep learning all he could about anything.

He walked into the parking lot of the gym looking at the cover of his magazines. A rover on Mars. He couldn't wait to see the pictures. Flipping through the pages he didn't notice all the people in parking lot looking up and pointing. He didn't notice the people running out of the buildings, then running back in to find cameras or camcorders.

The last thing he remembered was the picture on page 20 of a rock on a totally alien world.

4

Joel's consciousness finally took hold despite his best efforts to stay unconscious. He reluctantly admitted that he was awake but still refused to open his eyes. Little fingers of terror still played with his nerve endings and he fought to calm himself down.

Hard. He was laying on something hard. That much got through to his brain. It was also quiet, way too quiet if you asked him. He worked up the nerve to move his hand but he couldn't feel anything. After a moment he worked out that it was because his hand wasn't moving, it seemed frozen. The little terror fingers took a tighter grip.

Aliens always froze their victims. Then they probed and poked and then they would wipe his memory clean.

It was still quiet. He decided to risk opening his eyes. He felt for sure he could do it if he just tried hard enough. Slowly he opened them.

A low moan next to him caused them to slam shut again. The terror fingers now had a hold on his brain as well and he strangled out a whimper that would've made any six year old girl proud.

There was another moan, but this time it was followed by a voice. "Where the hell am I?" the voice said, with just a hint of anger in it.

A voice on the other side of him answered, "Who are you? What's going on?" This voice sounded somewhat disorientated. Joel whimpered again.

There were some grunts on both sides of him followed by the voices, almost in unison, saying, "Hey, I can't move."

Matt struggled on the table that he had woke up on. He looked over at the man on the table next to him. "Hey...hey, you. Do you know what's going on? I can tell you're awake, man, open your eyes." So far, all he could move was his head. He could see Joel on the next table squeezing his eyes shut.

"Is there somebody over there? What's going on?" Craning their necks, Matt and Gary caught a glimpse of each other.

"You got me, I think we're inside. I think we're inside that spaceship."

Gary looked around. The room was an oval about fifteen feet long and twelve feet wide. The walls were smooth as was the ceiling. The only things in the room were three tables with three men on them.

"What spaceship? What in god's name are you talking about?"

"The ship. You know, the flying saucer. It was hovering right over my fence."

They both paused and looked at Joel. "Hey, what's up with him?"

"I think he's scared." Matt said. "Hey, buddy, open your eyes. It's okay."

Joel forced his eyes open. At first he took in the smooth ceiling then looked one way, then the other. Then he lost it again.

"Oh, god, I can't move. It's all over. We're goners. They're gonna shove probes up our asses, shove needles in our balls, oh, god, I gotta get out of here." He shook his head, the only part of his body he could move, back and forth in a futile effort to free himself from the table.

"Whoa, calm down. Who's going to do this? What's going on?"

Joel looked over at Gary. "The aliens, man. Didn't you see them? They flew right over my car. Jeeze, it's just like on TV, they'll put us through tests…"

"Calm down."

"…poke needles in our eyes…"

"Will you be quiet?"

"…and god knows what…"

Suddenly a voice filled the room.

"Welcome." It said, in a smooth calming tone. Joel answered it with a high pitched scream. Matt and Gary both rolled their eyes.

After Joel had finished Matt looked over at him. "Will you cut that out? Let's just find out what's going on." He wanted to yell at him but all that came out was a loud whisper.

The voice spoke again. "Welcome to our ship. For your convenience, this is a recorded announcement. We will be with you shortly, after your implants have been calibrated."

"Oh god oh god oh god…" Joel banged his head on the table. "They already got me. I'm a goner for sure. Oh god oh god…"

Matt was getting angry. Gary was happy to just let Matt deal with it. "Will you please SHUT UP!" he yelled.

Joel closed his eyes. "Okay, I'm calm."

Gary put in a word of advice. "Just pull yourself together."

"You don't see us panicking." Matt lifted his head up and looked at Gary. "Matt, my names Matt."

Gary nodded at him. "Gary."

Joel took a few deep breaths. "Joel. Joel Martin. Sorry, sorry I feel better now."

Another voice seemed to penetrate the room. This voice was mechanical, and spoke in halting, broken sentences.

"Hello.
I...you...understanding...I...Mark...Mark..."

The three exchanged glances.

"This...you...understand...question...su perior understanding now?"

Matt was the first to speak up. "We understand you, kinda. Do you speak English?"

There was a moment of silence.
"Hello...English saying yes...with us...speak

slowly…with us we…understanding…" Again there was a pause. "You are…alrighty…dokey?"

Gary choked back a chuckle. "I guess," he said, with a hint of sarcasm, "but we can't move. Can you release us?" He flashed a grin around, hoping the voice would see it.

This time the pause was longer. Just before Matt was going say something the voice came back.

"Move…you will…not now but…later. Patience we ask. Safe…safety…only few minutes…then…you can toilet…wait…patience."

Matt frowned slightly. "Now that you mentioned it…"

"Please wait…us return…small…time."

"Oh god," Joel moaned again, "Now they're gonna film us on the toilet. What kind of sick aliens are these?"

"If you don't knock it off," Said Matt, "I'm going to smack you."

5

It was just a few moments later that the three men were able to start moving their limbs and a few moments after that when they were able to sit up. Their whole bodies went through that tingling sensation you get when your leg goes to sleep.

They checked out the wall which was smooth and cool. No breaks or cracks could be found and it seemed seamless where it met the floor and ceiling. Each table was on a single pedestal and easily slid around when pushed. For the most part they were quiet with only a few paranoid babblings from Joel.

"Wow, I don't even remember seeing a spaceship." Gary said. "Did you guys actually see any aliens?"

Matt looked at Joel, who was still examining the walls. "No. But the whole thing seemed too small to hold a room like this. And this air…it smells, well, it smells funny."

"It's pure." Gary said. "It's just like the isolation booth at the center. Filtered, extra oxygen added. I've had some great ideas in there."

Matt raised his eyebrow. "Isolation booth? Like what hippies use?"

Gary smiled. "Hippies? No, I just like to stay fit, try new things."

"In a moment you'll wish you never tried this." Joel was still pacing up and down the wall, looking for anything. "This room is sealed, we're gonna run out of air, purified or not." He slapped his hand on the wall. "Hellooooo. You can let us go now."

The answering voice caused Joel to jump on a table.

"Hello. This is better, no? You understanding more? Better?"

Matt whispered to Gary, "Sounds like Ruskies."

"Welcome aboard Tub. Feeling okay, you?"

"We're fine." Matt answered. "We'd like to know what's going on."

There was a pause. "We have…job…for you. We will speak of that time not now. In a…moment…we will…open door." The voice was still halting, as if it had to think of the proper words to say.

Joel got down and stood close to the other two. Too close. "What door, I wonder. Brace yourselves, they may come out firing."

Matt took a deep breath. "Will you please stop that? They may come out with a million dollars. For all we know we're on candid camera or something."

"Yeah, candid camera in the twenty-first century, maybe." Even Joel didn't know what he meant by that. The other two just looked back at him with narrowed eyes.

At that moment there was large clanking, gonging sound. Then, slowly, the wall separated from the floor and began to rise. On the other side was a large room, about the size of a football field, with a ceiling only about eight feet high. It was prefect for creating a very claustrophobic feeling.

It was filled with stuff. There was just no other way to describe it. At first glance it looked like a warehouse. They could see furniture, bicycles, building supplies, large picture frames, appliances, and countless boxes stacked around the walls, which were exactly like the one that was just lifted away. They took a few steps forward.

For the first time Joel relaxed. "This can't be a spaceship. Those TVs are Sonys. And why would an alien want a Ford Bronco? And…" He stopped when something caught his eye. "Are those arcade machines?" He left the group to check it out.

"Are you still there?" Matt shouted.

"Yes."

"Are those porta-potties functional?"

Again, a pause. "Yes. They are there for your…convenience. Better…arrangements…are coming. Everything you need will be…provided."

This time it was Gary who spoke up. "What do you mean? Did we win the lottery or something?"

There was long pause and Matt shrugged his shoulders and went off to relieve himself. After a few moments the voice came back.

"There will be more coming. This…storage…is one of several. You are on Tub."

At that Joel walked back over to Gary. "What? Do you mean we're really on a spaceship?"

"Yes."

"Then what's all this stuff for?" Joel's eyes got a size bigger. "I get it. It's for a museum or something. And we're part of it." He started to get agitated again. "We're gonna be sold at some cosmic garage sale..."

For the first time the voice interrupted. "No. You are...mistaken. This is yours. What you...do not see...but what you want...we will...retrieve...for you."

Gary leaned towards Joel, who was standing there with his jaw hanging. "Maybe," he whispered, "they think we're gods." He smiled, but Joel took him seriously.

"I don't get it." He said. "What do we have to do?"

"Please," the alien voice answered, "Make yourselves...comfortable. Food is here." A light started blinking on one wall, but where it came from, no one could tell. "Cooking...utensils...there. Arrange comfortable. When ready, we will talk."

"Just how long do you plan on keeping us here?"

"We will talk when…ready. Meantime, we will…fix…translation. Will work better. See you in…time."

Matt came out and approached the others. He was still hiking up his jeans. "Well, what'd I miss?"

6

"Bacon!" Joel said, "Look at all the bacon. I haven't had a good bacon sandwich in a long time."

They had found three large walk-in refrigerators and three even larger freezers. Joel and Matt were ohing and ahing over all their favorite foods while Gary was happy eating an apple and some bananas.

"That stuff will kill you, man." He said. "I think we should spend less time cooking and more time finding a way out of here." He looked at his watch. "We've been here 12 hours which means we were unconscious for at least 11. Now I've going to miss one of the most important meetings in my life and I want a damn good explanation for it. Personally, I don't believe we're in any UFO. Where ever we are, I think we're on Earth, and there has to be a way out."

"Well, UFOs or no, I'm starving. And frankly, I can't think that anybody who goes out of their way to get all this stuff can't be half bad. The guy said he had a job for us, and it looks to me that we're gonna get paid very well."

They eventually cooked their respective meals and ate at a large round table that was near the kitchen area. Matt seemed more relaxed than anybody and sat back with his feet on the table. As time passed Gary became more and more agitated. He felt like his life was slowly slipping away with each passing minute and wanted to salvage what was left of his career. He imagined trying to tell his bosses that he missed the meeting because he spent all day in a spaceship eating bacon and playing arcade games. Joel seemed more at ease but it was hard to tell. To the others he seemed hyperactive, jumping from item to item, oogling the quality of this thing or berating the quality of another.

All the while the men learned more about each other. When they discovered that all three of them came from completely different parts of the country they had to give a second thought to the fact that they really were on a spaceship.

A full three hours had passed and Matt was just ready to doze off on a large, comfy couch, when a new voice introduced itself. This voice seemed more human and less mechanical and was much smoother than the previous voices.

"Welcome aboard my starship. I am the…captain…of this vessel." The voice became slightly lower, almost a whisper. "It's still hesitating. Oh, that much is normal? Oh, I see." The voice rose to conversation level again. "Apparently our translator is working normally now. I wanted to make sure it was working before we met face to face to avoid any…problems. I know humans can be alarmed at strange things and I do not believe you have seen anything like us before." The voice almost seemed to chuckle. "Did you enjoy your eating?"

The three glanced at each other. "Well, yes we did, thank-you."

"Good. There are, of course, other holds with more food. Enough to last quite a long time. We will make more arrangements later, we don't want to forget anything."

There was a short pause. "Well, my human specialist assures me that this is as good a time as any to meet. The door is at the other end where you first came in." Again the voice lowered. "They're amazing looking. How do they keep from falling over? What? Release what button? Oh…" Then it cut off completely.

***

The men made their way to where the three tables still stood where they had originally awakened. They stood there in their thoughts, each trying to image what it was that could have possibly brought them together.

Then a small section of wall began to rise, or more accurately, began to disappear from the bottom, until the three men stood face to face with three aliens.

There was no mistaking that these were aliens. Nothing in any sci-fi flick had ever looked like this. Each stood about five feet tall at the tallest point, which changed when they moved. All three men thought that the aliens looked like giant orders of curly fries.

The bodies, about the size of a bean-bag chair, were made up of a tangle of, well it was hard to describe. It looked like a tangle of arms with no end and no beginning. The skin, if that's what it was, had the texture of deep-fried potatoes--golden brown and crispy. The whole mess was covered with what looked like a blanket with tassels around the edges. Out of this tangled mess three legs dropped down, two in front and one in back, that ended with what looked like golden-brown miniature elephant's feet. Out of the sides of the 'body' rose two stalks, again very arm-like in thickness and the way they had elbow-type bends, on top of which was clearly two eyes each, for a total of four, but not the kind of eyes seen on any Earth creature. Out of the middle in the front rose a much smaller stalk with a mouth on the end. It was moist and red inside but no teeth could be seen. Hanging at the sides, just behind the eye stalks, were two shorter stalks with six finger-like tentacles at the end. Trying to follow any of the arm, legs, eyes, or mouths into the tangle of the body was fruitless as you would immediately get lost in the thick tangles.

These creatures had obviously followed a completely different evolutionary path.

The alien in the middle had what looked like a backpack on its back but the other two just had the blankets, which hung almost all the way to the floor. There was also a small circle of cloth around each rear leg.

Another curious thing was the smell. It was almost as if the air was cleaner and fresher near the aliens or if there was actually an absence of smell near them. It was a pleasant sensation.

For a long time the two species just stood and stared at each other. Then the alien in the middle spoke.

"Hello," he said, but the sound came from the backpack. Although the mouth moved, no sound at all came out. "I am the captain of this vessel. Welcome aboard. My name is Bob."

The men just stood there until Matt voiced what they were all thinking. "Is your name really Bob?"

Gary's jaw finally dropped as his thoughts finally reeled out of control. "It's real," he said, barley breathing, "the whole thing is real. You're really an alien. A life form from a totally alien world."

The alien named Bob was speechless.

Gary looked around at the walls, half expecting them to start closing in on him like his brain was. "Then this really is a spaceship."

"Yes," said Bob, "We tried to name it but the translation programs kept translating the names as simply 'Tub. Our personal names translated into common Earth names, but the ship, oh no, it just wouldn't work."

For once Joel felt in control of himself. Here he was, surrounded by name-brand merchandise in a big warehouse, and was expected to believe this was real. Sure, the walls were cool and the aliens, well, they were a work of art but this couldn't be real. He could have come up with better aliens than this, he thought.

Bob's features got a little bit straighter, it was almost like a human trying to stand taller. "We would like to solicit your help in a momentous undertaking."

One of the other aliens step forward and spoke. The men could see his mouth move but the voice still came from the back-pack on the middle alien, although it was clearly a different voice. "Yes, a very momentous undertaking.

We need your help in a big way. Did that translate right?"

Matt was still distracted. "You know, if we could prove you exist, we'd be millionaires."

"Yeah," Gary added, "I mean, this would be the biggest thing to hit mankind since, well, since..."

"Since buttered bread." Matt finished.

"I'm still not sure about this." Joel said, stepping closer to the aliens. "There's got to be strings or wires or something. I could've come up with better aliens than these."

Matt and Gary looked at Joel. Was this the same whimpering college student they met half a day before? "It's real, man." Matt said. "This isn't a joke. This is incredible, that's what it is." He hiked his jeans up again, wondering if it would be out of place to tighten his belt at this point.

All the while Bob was trying to follow their conversation. "I think we have...gotten off the point."

"Oh yeah," Joel said. "This big favor. What could an advanced race of aliens want from three total strangers? What's so special about us?"

The third alien finally spoke. Again, the voice from the pack was different. "Nothing is special about you. You were chosen at random." He glanced at the other two aliens. "Almost." He added, after they glanced back.

Gary shook his head to try and shake loose the thoughts that were lodged there. "We're really in a spaceship with aliens." He started nodding, and had to hold back the urge to laugh. This was the happiest moment of his life. He, above the other two, realized the implications of the human race finally meeting another race from another planet. It was what every science geek dreamed about. It almost seemed his whole life passed before his eyes, from watching specials on TV with blurry photos of something that was almost, but not quite, a flying saucer to reading Cosmos by Carl Sagan and following every step of the latest Mars mission. He couldn't wait to get one of these creatures to the press, hopefully before the government got involved, although he never really believed the government would go ape over an alien and do anything to cover it up. Through all the scientific implications of this moment, all he could say was, "This is sooo cool!"

The smile melted from Joel's face. It was if he could feel the electricity coming off of Gary. "This is real, isn't it?"

The second alien looked at Bob. "Bob, I think we are forgetting that these people have never discovered life off of their own world. This must be very exciting for them."

Gary nodded, almost violently. "It is. It's very exciting."

Bob pointed behind the men. "Please, let us get comfortable, then we can talk. I guess you will have many questions, and we need your help in a big way."

All six of them felt lightheaded as they headed for the couches.

7

John looked out the window at the strange stars that dotted the universe.

Of course, he didn't know his name was John. That was just the proper name the translation entity picked for him.

He said the command to keep the window open as he looked away. Normally, it would vanish if there was no one looking out it but John wanted it to be there when he looked back.

A creepy, tingly sensation ran through his coils as he wandered around his cabin, wondering what was going on so far beneath him. He couldn't believe they were actually on his ship. Well, THE ship, anyway. He always thought of it as his own even though it was communally owned by all those aboard it. He had served here the longest and he knew every inch of it like the back of his own eyes.

He couldn't stand those things, those humans. Big bags of water and bones held together with a single skin, like a giant balloon. His own body, if you looked at it close enough, was tiny strands twisted into each other in larger and larger bundles until the bundles were large enough to support eyes, arms, and legs. He was much sturdier than most life on Earth, each tiny strand expendable. He knew that soon there would be a whole group of them on board, breathing and eating and drinking and excreting like big machines. Or like big, water-filled balloons, the thought wouldn't leave his thought center.

God, he hoped one of them didn't pop. He hated seeing that red liquid flow out of them as they deflated. No liquid flowed through his body unless he was submersed in it, which reminded him that he was hungry. He would go down to the vats and take a quick dip in some nutrients and then find a control room, probably his favorite one. Especially for this occasion.

He had to say goodbye to his ship.

8

Matt, Gary, and Joel watched with a little embarrassment as three aliens named Bob, Joe, and Kevin cleared off their seats, which were mistaken for small end tables earlier. The aliens simply straddled them then rested on them crossing their legs in front of them which made them appear strangely human. You could just picture them sticking their hands in their blue jeans and leaning back against a wall.

But, of course, they physically couldn't.

Bob pulled himself up straight and looked at the three humans in front of him, thinking how they crossed their legs looked strangely familiar.

"I think this is the time to explain ourselves to you."

Rather than reply, the men just sat there, waiting.

"We are called Gorgons. I don't know how the translator will translate that but there it is. We are explorers and have come across a great many planets that are just teeming with life, but there are not many with civilizations and certainly none that are spacefarers as we. With the exception of one."

Joe leaned forward. "The Gorgons."

Matt looked at each of the aliens. "I thought you said you were the Gorgons."

"We are." Said Bob, his eyestalks wavering a bit. "I think it translated wrong. Try Minks. There I think that translated correctly. I apologize to you. Our translation entity was grown by the lowest bidder. I tried to get a better one but it was out of my hands."

"Lowest bidder?"

Alien Kevin spoke up. "Yes, when I studied your planet I found that your economy was very similar to our own, and passed that information on to the translator so you should be hearing an accurate translation in this area."

The men nodded, then Bob went on.

"The Minks were very angry that we visited their planet. They were as advanced as we were but chose not to be spacefarers. We tried to make peace but they invaded our space with devastating biological weapons. Battles continue to be fought but they are by chance. It is as if they are just taking occasional pot-shots at us, to remind us to stay away. It has been difficult because they are hitting us harder each time."

After a pause Joe started in. "The upshot is that we can no longer support our population. Their weapons were not aimed at destruction, but at our plant life. One biological bomb can kill plant life in an entire ocean for centuries. In base terms, we are starving."

Joel perked up and those late night shows where humans were used as food flooded back into his brain.

"We are not in jeopardy yet, however." Bob added. "As I said, we visited many planets and have found a few that we can grow plenty of food on. The location of these are now one of our biggest secrets."

"So, what do you need us for?" Gary said, his curiosity bouncing around his brain like a ping-pong ball in a tornado. He wished that they would get to the point.

Joe continued. "We need you to, well to..."

He looked at Bob for help. Bob knew he was in charge, so it was up to him. "We need farmers. You see, we cannot breathe on these planets. Of course, we don't breathe the same way you do."

"Think of our breathing as one long, continuous inhale. We exhale as well, but only when we have to." Kevin said.

Everybody seemed lost. Then Kevin spoke up again. "Don't get us wrong, you could not breathe there, either, but your children can."

All three men explained that they had no children.

"You don't understand. We have not gotten to the favor yet." Started Bob. "But I think Kevin can explain it better."

"Well, we knew enough about you to modify your bodies to breathe this atmosphere but we cannot alter you enough to breathe on those planets with the fertile seas. But we can alter your genes enough so when you have children, they will be able to breathe on this planet. You would not even notice that they are different in any way."

Gary was already waving his hands, beating Matt and Joel to the burning question. "Hold on a minute. What do you mean you modified our bodies?"

"Only slightly. There is no oxygen in this atmosphere. If we did not alter you a little, you would suffocate." Even though they were very alien to him, he could see them getting upset. "It was a very minor change."

"That's impossible. Then what are we breathing?"

"A complex mixture of many things, it would take hours to explain. It was a very minor change, mere molecules."

Gary and the others were still in disbelief. "You mean you can change just a few molecules in our bodies, and we can breathe differently?"

"Well, a few molecules in every cell in your body. And it wasn't easy. There were microbes as well. And we modified many of your supplies..."

Gary stood up but was too dizzy so he sat back down. Joel was staring at his hands, almost through them, trying to spot the change. A few molecules in every cell had to change something.

Matt just leaned back. "So, you want us to be farmers?"

Bob glanced at his companions. "No, you misunderstand. We want your children to be the farmers. What we are asking of you is to have the children."

Joel stopped looking at his hands and started laughing. "Boy, do we need to explain a few things to you."

Kevin spoke up again. "I think you still do not understand. You will each have 10 females that will bear the children. There will be other ships starting other, well, let's call them colonies. Then, all your children, and their children, by this time grown in full adults, will be transferred to the farming planets. We are talking about thousands to prevent certain genetic problems. And we will be there to cater to your every need. You will not have to do anything."

Joel smiled. "Except breed."

Bob sat up straight. "Exactly."

Matt was shaking his head. "You have just got to be shitting me."

All three aliens straightened their eyestalks, a sign of surprise.

"I do not think that translated properly." Said Bob. "It would be physically impossible to do that. Plus, we do not eat the same way you do."

Gary shook his head. "He means your joking. You're kidding. You want groups of three men and thirty women to have kids so they can work for you on another planet? We don't do things that way. Why didn't you come down and ask for volunteers? You would've gotten a lot. Why us?"

"Well," Bob said, "not all humans can be modified. And we were afraid. We announced ourselves to the Minks and now we have enemies. No, it was decided that we do this in the way we have done it. Pick three men, let them pick 10 women, and go with it."

Matt leaned forward. "And if we don't want to?"

Bob slumped. "I don't know. But you cannot go back. We cannot undo what we have done. You would suffocate in your own atmosphere."

"I can't believe it." Joel said. "It's like we're being shanghaied to mate."

9

It was obviously a sleepless night for the men. Kevin, it was explained, would be a sort of liaison between the aliens and the humans and any needs would be directed to him. They were left alone in the storeroom although it was explained that there were two more just like it, one for each man, and many more general stores on top of that.

"I'm not going for it." Gary was saying, eating some more the best fruit he had ever tasted. "I want out. I don't like the fact that we've been kidnapped."

Joel was leaning forward, trying to get the bacon sandwich he had concocted to drip on a plate. "Oh, come on. We're escaping from the rat race, with ten beautiful love slaves to boot. Bob said we'd be catered to for the rest of our lives. We'll be on a whole alien world. We'll be heroes to an entire race."

Matt finally spoke up from his fourth bowl of cereal. "Yeah, but what's that if you can't share it. I mean, for you it's easy, no family, no ties. I'm engaged to be married. I have a brother and a father and a farm to take care of. I want kids, but I want them with Melody. I want them to know my dad. But then again, not to agree with everything you're saying," he pointed with his spoon towards Joel, "I don't mind helping out where I can, and these...whatever they are, seem to be desperate."

Gary heaved a heavy sigh. "But you're not seeing the big picture here. It's not just us. Thirty women are going to be uprooted just like we were. Kidnapped. No word to their families, no choice, no, well, just no nothing. I don't like it and..."

"And what?"

"Well, just I don't like it."

For a few moments the only sounds heard were the munching and slurping of the three men. Joel was the first to see Kevin standing in the corner, part of the wall gone without a trace.

"We have a visitor."

Kevin walked up to the three men, wearing the backpack that Bob had worn earlier. "Forgive the intrusion. There is something I thought you might like to see."

For the first time since they came on board, the men were led from the storage area. The hallway was long and smooth which was no surprise given the nature of the doors on the ship. At no particular point that anyone could tell Kevin stopped and a door opened in the wall, but smaller than any they had seen so far. Inside was a small semi-circular room with no features whatsoever. It held the four of them with maybe room for four more.

"Don't be alarmed, it's just a window." Before anyone could comment on this, the wall, floor, and ceiling vanished. At first Joel, Gary, and Matt stumbled with the loss of perspective. Then, when they had regained their footing, they saw it. It was a tiny, blue dot, but there was no mistaking the Earth. It was breathtaking to see it just hanging there in space, so tiny. No one dared to breathe.

After a few minutes, or hours, Gary spoke. "We're really here."

Kevin spoke, and even the backpack seemed to whisper. "That's it. Imagine, the entire human race, all of its people, all of its accomplishments, all its habitats, are on that tiny sphere." There was again a long silence. "Our world looks much the same from space. It only took one missile to make it inhospitable. We can't even feed ourselves on our own planet anymore. We need you."

Matt looked at Kevin. "You don't think..."

"You are our best kept secret. That's why we came here in a small ship, that's why we're doing all this the way we are."

It was at that point that they looked up and down. The ship was terribly hard to see because it was as black as the space around it. They could see some other semi-circular protrusions here and there but only barely. It was just a great black mass behind them.

"This is a tiny ship?"

"By our standards, yes."

Shaken to his senses, Gary started looking harder at the Earth. "Where's the moon?"

Kevin pointed farther away than any of them would have guessed. It took them a few moments to pick it out from the stars.

"Who would've guessed? It's like that thing they show you in school where the Earth is a pea and the moon is a...a...smaller pea."

Gary and Matt looked at Joel. Matt said, "You know, he's right."

Gary silently admitted that he remembered those lectures the same way.

They once again fell silent and stared at the Earth some more. It was strangely hypnotic seeing it hang there all alone in space. Matt tried to imagine Melody and his family down there, insignificant nothings on a tiny speck.

Before he could stop himself, "I'm in. I'm going to do it."

Joel looked at him, "What?"

"I'm in. I'll do it. I'll help the..." he looked at Kevin, he could hardly believe he could say the word, it sounded so corny. "The Gorgons."

Kevin's eyestalks went straight, the equivalent of a smile.

"I think I can do this. I think I need to. What has the Earth to offer my kids? I can do something, achieve something."

Even Joel saw something at that moment. "I see what you mean. I don't think that I would ever do anything as good on Earth. Maybe I could come back some day."

Gary still couldn't be swayed. "The Earth is a beautiful place. I would be proud to raise my kids there."

Matt chuckled. "Just a few days ago, I didn't know there was any other place to raise them. Or any other way."

"There's an entire universe out there." Kevin said. "And all of us will be eternally in your debt." After a few more moments he added, "Just go back down the hall the way we came, your door will be open and will close when you go through." And with that he left.

Joel stepped forward and pressed against the invisible wall. "I could stay here forever."

10

Kevin put his translator in a communal storage locker and went to absorb nutrients at the location he was told. Waiting was John, a wise old Gorgon, and no one else.

"Well?" asked John.

Kevin stepped into the pool where he would absorb what he needed for the day. When he spoke it was in his own voice, his own language, far below the level any human could hear. "They are extraordinary beings. Already you can see them listening, watching, adapting..."

"We've never found anything like them."

"No, but as adaptive as they are, they are also strong-willed. One is still resisting."

"Then kill him"

"No, then we would have to start all over. The other two would never cooperate if we killed one." Kevin twisted each pair of eyes in on themselves, a sort of smile. "There's nothing to worry about, they know they can't go back now. They'll pick their mates and we'll be on our way."

"And Bob?" John also crossed each pair of eyes.

"Is doing everything he can to make sure his mission goes as planned."

"Then let's just be sure our mission goes as planned as well."

Kevin knew his place and his elder as well. He got out and stood under a dryer for a few seconds and uncrossing one pair of eyes, left.

John stayed, savoring the nutrients he was absorbing as slowly as he could. He slouched down so that only his eyes were above the green liquid, a vulgar move had other Gorgons been present. But alone he didn't care. He was assuring himself that his mission was going as planned as well and hoping there weren't too many more plans to worry about.

But he dismissed that as nonsense. Who could have a higher plan than he?

His mouth poked up out of the liquid and gave the command that locked the door. Then, in a move that would have disgusted even the rudest of Gorgons, he closed his eyes and went all the way under.

11

It was a long time before anyone spoke again, but the silence was broken by Gary. "I wonder how far away we are."

Nobody said anything, so he continued. "I was supposed to go to Brazil. It's funny, I was looking forward to traveling, to going to South America. I wanted to explore, to visit some ruins."

"I wonder if we could stop at Mars, you know, dance in front of that little rover thing. Wouldn't that be a hoot?" Joel was smiling at the thought.

There was again silence for a long while. Matt looked at Gary. "You really don't want this, do you?"

Without hesitation, "No."

"This is something that every man dreams about, at least sometimes. Flying to the stars, visiting another world."

"You know," said Gary, "This reminds me of a story. When I first went to Colorado I spent a couple of weeks hiking in the mountains. I saw this one mountain, it wasn't too big, it wasn't too small. I'd never climbed a mountain before but this one had long, gentle slopes leading up to a flat peak. It was mid-morning and I was just staring at it, wondering how long and how hard it would be to climb it. An old Indian just came out of nowhere and

looked with me. He asked me what I was
staring at."

Gary's voice got a little bit lower. "I
know it seemed crazy, but I told him about a
dream I had where I saw this very same
mountain. I really did have it. It all kinda came
to me at that time. Well, he told me I had to
climb it. He said my spirit lived on the peak and
if I never climbed the mountain then I would
never truly be at one with my spirit. I told him I
was ill equipped to climb at that moment and he
said I had to do it that day, or I might miss my
spirit."

"What'd you do?"

Gary took a deep breath. "Well, I
climbed it. It took all day and I nearly wore
through the soles of my poor tennis shoes. All I
had was a canteen of water and my own will. I
reached the top right at sunset. It looked like all
the mountains were on fire. I'd never seen
anything so beautiful in my entire life. I think
he was right, I did find my spirit on that
mountain. Nothing was ever the same after that.
I took real control of my life, lived for the
moment. I actually spent the night up there. I
could actually touch the stars."

Matt, who had sat down, nodded his head. "It must have looked something like this."

"Not really. I mean this is unreal, it's beautiful, you can really see the constellations out here, like nothing you can see on Earth. But that night the constellations seemed to come alive, to talk to me. The next day I tried to find that old man, to thank him."

"Let me guess." Joel said, "Everybody said you described someone who died years before."

"No," Gary shrugged, "They told me he had wandered away from a home. He was really from LA and told everyone he was an old Indian chief even though anyone doubted he had any Indian in him at all. That didn't change anything, though. I was eternally grateful to him. I still stop in to see him when I get the chance."

"I don't think you'll get the chance anymore."

"That's just it. I want the chance. I think my spirit is still on that little ball out there and I will not be whole again until I'm back. That's my next big challenge in life - to get home."

"I hate to tell you this, mate," Joel said, putting his hand on Gary's shoulder, "But I think you're hopelessly outmatched this time. We're at the mercy of these aliens now and I think we ought to take what we can while we can. We can't go home again, so why fight it?"

Matt looked up at the other two. "I just hope they're being honest with us. If everything they say is true, then we're set for life."

"And if they're not?"

"Well, let's just hope they are. I've jumped off the barn before, but this drop's a doosie."

12

The men spent the next couple of days getting acquainted with their surroundings. Kevin and Bob each spent some time with them and showed them some of the other holds which were filled with the very best Earth had to offer. At least that's what the aliens thought.

All three were given what looked like remote control devices which could drop walls, open doors and windows, and even translate in a pinch although Kevin explained it was a very rudimentary translator. Most Gorgons that were going to interact with the humans would carry one like Kevin wore. He told them about the ship and the two hundred and twenty five Gorgons that made up her crew. Most of them were in research, he explained, as the ship basically ran itself. Kevin was head of Human Research and asked endless questions trying to clarify even the most trivial matters, like why do humans shave their face, or what a tie was for.

When alone, Gary tried his best to convince his comrades not to buy in to all the hype but it was hard when Joel kept finding things he had always wanted, like high end cameras and video arcade games. Matt and Gary even left him alone for hours in one of the holds and when they came back they found him watching Laurel and Hardy movies on a big screen TV, complete with a case of potato chips and another case of Pepsi. Walkman stereos were laying on the couch and floor around him and DVDs were strewn everywhere.

"I found the Earth movie archive." he explained.

Matt was feeling kind of comfortable. He never wanted much out of life but inside he felt just like Joel. The thought of spending the rest of his life with all his needs tended for and not having to work for it sent chills down his spine. He was especially pleased when he asked how much farming equipment was on board and found out there was none. Kevin got agitated that they may have overlooked something but Matt assured them that none of it was needed.

Yes, thought Matt, these guys mean to please.

Gary, on the other hand, was bent on gathering information. He questioned Kevin almost as much as Kevin questioned him but tried to make it seem like simple curiosity. He purposefully spaced out the important questions while throwing in mundane questions to try to keep any pattern from forming. He learned that there were emergency capsules on board, each able to hold five passengers comfortably, but in the history of the Gorgons no ship ever failed enough to use them. He also learned that the Gorgon ship had been in orbit around the Earth-moon system for almost a year and had spent that time rigorously gathering information. They had been here before, but it was unclear as to how long ago that was, Kevin mentioned it was in his grandmother's time and humans were just starting to form cities. Gary knew he'd have come back to this because it would be a great opportunity to learn some history. Maybe there actually were some ancient aliens.

Gorgons, Gary found, were like humans when it came to technology--everybody used it but no one knew how it worked. He was becoming frustrated with the number of times Kevin answered a question with "I'm not sure how it works, but we've been using it for years." He also couldn't discern what type of command structure there was, if any. Bob was captain, and Kevin headed a group of researchers and there were a few other groups, but it was confusing as to who was in charge of who or if indeed anyone was superior to anyone else. Kevin would at times mention receiving an order from Bob but at other times mention that he gave Bob an order. Gary had decided the only way to learn for certain was to come right out and ask Kevin, but figured it wasn't time yet. He wanted to learn more about the ships that went to Earth to pick up supplies, and people, and where he could find one.

As usual, Kevin seemed almost ignorant of them, almost like someone who knew how to drive a car, but had never seen or heard of the engine that lay under the hood.

Then it happened, and Joel got to go first.

13

The room was almost exactly the same as the one they had first awakened in, only this time it was long enough for ten tables. Gary was pacing furiously and Matt was leaning against the entrance. Joel was also pacing, but out of anticipation and had to keep dodging Gary.

"I can't believe you're going through with this. You can help me, you know."

"Sure I could, Gary, but then if we really are stuck here then I'd be stuck with a bunch of old, fat broads."

It was Gary's intention to recruit some help to get off the ship. He scoured some magazines and newspapers until he had what he thought was a perfect mix of biochemists, scientists, psychologists, and even a pilot to help form a way to get off the ship. He wanted more, but the 10 women limit prevented him from getting everyone he wanted.

Joel had his own way to pick his ten women.

"I can't believe you went with one calendar." Matt put in. "Just one calendar. And you think they're gonna find these women from just a picture?"

"Well, what's-his-name, Kevin's assistant, said they could. Said it was no problem. And in just a few minutes they're gonna be right here. Poor Miss December, too bad Santa outfits are such a turn off."

"Who else did you leave off?"

"Miss January, too much winter wear, I just couldn't see what I was getting."

"Dammit, Joel." Yelled Gary. "These are women, not possessions. And I doubt very much they'll have anything to do with you. Especially after you kidnap them away from their homes, their loved ones."

"I might remind you," Joel started, trying to sound smug, "That in a few hours you will be doing the same."

"Yes, but at least I'm picking women who can appreciate the situation. These are aliens from another world, the most historic thing since Jesus. And I have no plan whatsoever to mate with them."

"You'd better hope not, some of your women are in their sixties. Let's hope the Gorgons haven't figured out biological clocks yet."

"At least when we get back to Earth I'll be known as the one that helped us escape. You'll be known as the one who tried to take advantage of the situation for having sex. Then who's going to look stupid?"

Before Joel could answer the long wall went up. Ten Gorgons pushing ten tables entered the room, then backed out. The wall went back down.

Matt stood up straight and gawked. Gary shook his head. Joel was frozen.

"Well, I gotta say," said Matt, "You sure can pick 'em." He trailed off.

Joel walked up and down the tables slowly. He couldn't convince himself that this was real. Here lay ten gorgeous women and they were all his.

As if he could read Joel's thoughts, Gary said, "They're not yours, you know. These are prisoners, and good luck dealing with them."

He used his remote to make a door and went back into the ship. Before the door went down, Matt followed.

"Good luck." He said with a wave.

Before the door lowered to the floor Joel became terrified. "Wait…"

It shut. He was alone. He wondered if anyone was watching. A very uncomfortable feeling was setting in. This was real, he had really stole ten women from Earth and now he had to tell them why.

He bent over the closest woman. She didn't appear to be one of the ten he picked. Going through the calendar in his mind he tried to match her up to a month. Now she looked a little familiar. He went through the same thing with the next girl, then the next. They sure looked different in real life.

At the last table he decided to get a little brave. Very slowly he reached out and put his hand on her shoulder, then jerked it back. He reached out again and this time left it there and very gently gave her a little shake. He wanted to explore her whole body but figured that half the ship was watching at this point.

She didn't stir. How long did Kevin say they'd be out? A few minutes, he thought. The girl moaned and Joel jerked his hand back and fell against the wall. This was supposed to be the greatest moment of his life and he was scared as hell.

A movement caught his eye. Some of the women were starting to stir. Joel moved to the center of the room and waited nervously. He had been going over his speech in his head and was wondering if they were awake enough hear him. How could he tell when the moment was right?

He cleared his throat. Then one of the women started screaming.

Joel felt like he had been hit by lightning. Another woman started screaming then another. Without realizing it Joel, too, was up against the wall screaming. Soon the whole room was screaming and women started falling off the tables, flailing their arms, and kicking. It took several minutes for it to start dying down as some women came to their senses and started calming the rest down.

The last person screaming was Joel, who by now was all curled up in a ball in the far corner of the room. When he stopped and gathered the nerve to open his eyes and take the fists out of his ears he found ten very different faces glaring at him.

14

Fifteen Gorgons watched in bewilderment as Matt and Gary rolled on the floor laughing so hard that they nearly passed out. The Gorgons themselves were laughing, in their own way, with their eyes bobbing up and down and crossing.

"I am so glad you found that funny." Kevin was saying. His eyes kept crossing. "I am almost certain that is not the reaction Joel was looking for."

Matt was catching his breath. "No, I'm sure it wasn't. I'm so glad you guys saw the humor in that."

"At first I thought they were dying." This statement started a new round for Matt and Gary. "And then I though that you were. It's absolutely fascinating."

"Do you think it's safe to turn the sound back up?" Gary giggled. "Boy, he sure got what he deserved."

Kevin and the other Gorgons wasn't sure what that meant but they continued their completely silent laughter.

15

"Okay girls, okay…" Joel was saying, as he got up off the floor and pulled himself together. "There's a logical explanation for all of this. Now just calm down and let me speak."

It was very hard for the women to calm down and Joel could hardly believe they were all really here.

"You are all aboard an alien craft on a mission of much importance. The Gorgons need our help in populating a world so they can grow food and survive."

A very lovely blond started nodding sarcastically. "Gorgons? And you are?"

"Oh, my name is Joel, and you are my picks for mating." Then he instantly regretted saying it.

"Of all the nerve. If this isn't a hidden camera show I'm going to beat the crap out of you."

All the Gorgons watching pictured this with disgust.

All the women in the room agreed with the blond.

"That didn't come out right," Joel continued, being only slightly distracted by one woman who only wore a teddy. "What I mean is that you are my chosen ones to bear children for the Gorgons. Wait, that's not how it sounds…" Ten very beautiful women started closing in on him.

"Okay, let's start over. You really are on an alien ship. Let's just start there."

A brunette spoke up. "I believe him. I saw the UFO coming down at me. I was in a boat and didn't know what to do."

Another girl spoke up. "Me, too. I was in the commons at the school and it came right over the admin building."

Most of the women agreed they had seen something before they blacked out. Joel decided not to mention any mating and went with the alien angle. To prove at least part of it he opened the door to demonstrate the technology but Bob standing outside the door impressed them even more. Not realizing he was out there, Joel closed the door as a further demonstration just as Bob started talking.

"Feel this wall," he said, "There's not even a crack. Now that's not Earth technology." He looked at the mostly frozen faces. "What?"

The first blond spoke up. "There was something outside that door."

Joel turned and opened the door again. There stood Bob, Joe, and another Gorgon whose name he couldn't remember.

"This is Bob, he's the captain of the starship Tub."

Bob took a step forward. "Welcome. We have a room prepared where you can comfortably sit and then all will be explained."

His words were lost, however, to a totally new round of screaming.

It took a half an hour but with the help of the only other humans on the ship Joel was able to get the women seated in one of the holds that had been set up as kind of an auditorium. Of course, there were Laz-Y-Boys instead of fold out seats but nobody seemed to mind.

Bob explained the plight of the Gorgons and Kevin explained the atomic changes made to their bodies and the fact that it couldn't be reversed. Gary and Matt introduced themselves and Joel just stood back and let everyone else do the talking since they were so much better at it than he was.

The ten reactions could only be described as similar, but different.

"You sick freaks," the blond, now identified as Karen was saying. "You bastards kidnap us then expect us to bear your children and all the while be happy about it?"

Another woman, Annie, was breaking down. Sherri, sitting next to her was trying to comfort her. "I have a year old daughter and you're saying I'll never see her again? I have no idea what even has happened to her today. I love her so much and they're gonna think I abandoned her." With that realization she completely collapsed onto Sherri.

Karen stood up. "You see what you've done? Did you even think this through?"

Bob spoke up. "Yes, we do not want the governments of Earth to know anything about us. It may be too dangerous."

"There are already news reports of UFO abductions in broad daylight in front of hundreds of witnesses. And you don't want to be known?"

"There are calculated risks. And our lasso was not working properly. No one on your planet will ever know anything beyond that..."

Another girl, Amanda, was grinning at the whole discussion. "You guys, this is so exciting. Don't you see? There really are aliens and we're really on their ship..."

"I still think we're on very bad episode of Candid Camera." Yet another girl said.

"Will we be home soon? Because I have to get up early tomorrow."

"Kevin," Joel said quietly, "I think we need to show them the window."

Karen wasn't done. "Why us? Who on Earth picked us?"

The room turned very silent as Joel slowly raised his hand.

"Then you're the one I'm going to kill."

16

Hours later Kevin wandered the corridors of the ship looking for John. He found him in a remote part of the ship looking at a monitor that showed the interior of one of the holds.

"I am not sure that went well." Kevin said as he entered the small room. "The females were very resistant to coming on board."

"Let us hope the next collection goes a little bit better. We are exposing ourselves too much on this planet. If they ever find out where our mother ship is…"

"They can do nothing. They have no means of space travel and we can easily, very easily dodge whatever they throw at us from the surface."

John's eyestalks kept staring at the ten women now sitting by themselves in one of the holds. Many were quiet and thoughtful after seeing the Earth through the window. Some were pacing wildly and only one was making any food. The room had been transformed into a dormitory by the women even though there were holds already set up for that purpose.

They were not about to be separated and banded together in their own way.

This little change was not lost on John.

"Look at them." John said slowly. "Already they are adapting, changing their environment to meet their whims. With them nothing can go as planned, nothing is guaranteed."

Kevin stood up a little bit straighter. It was his job to make sure everything involving the humans went as planned and John's remarks were a sort of insult to his ability to do his job. He was, after all, the resident expert on humans.

"I can guarantee that they are survivors. They always find a way."

"Let us hope that they do not find their way too soon."

"Would like to meet them? You get a different feel for them when you are right there with the translator, watching their face change shapes…"

"Oh, no. They give me the creeps. I've got a good view from here, where it's safe."

Kevin chuckled himself with his eyes at the thought of a Gorgon being afraid of humans.

At least such a small group of harmless ones. He left John watching the hold and trotted back to speak to Joel. He wanted to know more about the reactions of the women so he could add it to his database. They were so different, the men and women. It was all so fascinating and he felt lucky that he got to research them so closely.

As he entered the storage section of the ship where all the holds were he ran into Bob and Matt talking in the hallway.

"Kevin," Matt said, through Bob's translator, "What do think of this idea?"

17

The three men were getting ready for bed in what was becoming known as The Men's Hold. The kitchen area was getting well used and they each had a bed in a different part of the football field sized room. They even found that their remotes let them put dividers up when they wanted to sleep.

"I wish I could help you," Matt was saying to Gary, "but I already gave that Gorgon, what's-his-name my list."

"Larry, he has the purple sash and one big ring near the rear."

"Yeah, Larry. And from what I'm told, he's already gone. If you would have come to me yesterday, I wouldn't have hesitated in the least. It's just too late now."

Joel was eating a bacon sandwich. "They are even more beautiful than I imagined." He sighed. "Too bad they won't let me into their room."

"It's criminal." Gary said, shaking his head. "You don't even know their names."

Joel shoved the last piece of sandwich in his mouth. "I will. It's just so unreal now that they're here. It's like…like…I don't know…"

"Like you've kidnapped ten beautiful women and now you realize that they'll have nothing to do with you and this whole Gorgon scheme is never going to work? Like you took a mother away from her baby and wives away from their husbands? Like now you're feeling a little shame at it all?"

"Oh, jeeze. I was just wondering how I was going to work a schedule out. Now I feel like shit. Who said they were married? They didn't look married."

"Quit being so hard on him." Matt put in. "I notice you had a list, too. You're in the same boat we're in."

"Yeah, but I'm getting the greatest minds of our time. Scientists, biologists, mechanical engineers, doctors. We're gonna find a way home. I even found an Air Force test pilot, in case we need to fly something."

"The Gorgons will never stand for that. At least some won't. I think Bob and Larry are okay." Matt got up to his feet. "And that one that tries to make jokes, and Kevin."

"I can't tell them apart. I hope they never change clothes or I'll be completely lost." Joel, too, was ready to turn in. But he knew that sleep was going to be hard to come by tonight. He had a lot to think about, or at least a lot to try not to think about.

He looked at the other two. "Do you think they'll be all right? I don't think they understand the big picture. It's not just about me, you know."

"Yeah, the Gorgons." Matt said, walking to his bed. "It'll be alright after they sleep on it, or at least after we sleep on it. My future wife will get here in a few days and I'll explain it to

her and she can calm them all down.
Everything will be…well, calmer at least."

With that the men went to their separate
spaces and almost simultaneously three little
cubicles rose out of the floor.

Joel lay awake for hours going through
every emotion that a human could possible go
through. They all fought in him, like some epic
battle that would determine the future of all
mankind. He was so busy having his every
dream come true that he didn't considered that
the women he chose would have a different
point of view. Regret wrestled with guilt for a
while, then anger and confusion. Slowly
heroism crept in as his selfishness waned and
the magnitude of the good deed that he involved
in grew in his mind. He was saving a whole
race, but then again he was taking the lives of
10 women.

Hopefully, and it was deep rooted hope,
they would see the logic of the situation and the
adventure that was about to take place. Hope
was the last thing he felt as he finally faded off
into sleep.

18

Karen sat alone on the edge of one of the couches that formed a big half circle and could sit all ten women comfortably except not all ten women were comfortable. At least one was sobbing uncontrollably and several were trying to comfort her and some others were just crying to themselves. Two or three sat alone and this is where Karen found herself.

She was thinking about her dad, and how furious he was when he found out she posed for that calendar. It would change her life, he said, and she was sure he had no idea how right he was. Without thinking she traced the scar that ran up her arm.

It was still fresh.

Smiling, she thought about what the others in ward must have thought when the UFO appeared outside the window. That was the last thing she remembered. Did she float out? Was she beamed up? Whatever happened she must have set the therapy of at least 20 people back many years.

The girl next to her was tearing up.

"Hey, Becky was it?" she asked as kindly as she could.

"Yeah," she answered, then with all the control she could muster added, "Miss April" and rolled her eyes.

"What did you get pulled from?"

Becky took a deep breath. "I was just coming out of the mall. Spent a small fortune on clothes. My boyfriend and I were going to go to Europe for a week. You?"

Karen tugged at her gown. "I was coming back from group. Was looking forward to my sleeping pill for the night."

"Were you in the hospital?"

"Yeah, kinda."

Becky raised her eyebrows, "Everything okay?"

"Just court ordered observation. I'm not sick or anything." Without actually showing her scars she made a point of making them visible to Becky.

They sat in silence for a while then Becky nudged Karen and nodded to the other side of the couch. "Is that girl praying?"

"Yeah, I wonder if god can hear us up here."

"I was thinking that, too." She nodded towards the sobbing girl. "She was shopping with her baby girl. Has no idea what happened to her."

"I'm glad I'm not that poor girl in her underwear, I wonder what got interrupted there?"

The two women smiled at one another. Although they didn't realize it they were both having the same thoughts.

Where ever they all came from, they are all in the same boat now.

"Hey," said Karen, looking over her shoulder to the vast hold behind them. "Let's see if we can find her some clothes."

"That sounds like a good idea."

For the first time in months, Karen forgot about the reason for her scars.

19

"I just want to try to explain this to you again." Gary was sitting on the edge of his chair talking with Kevin, who was listening intently. "Humans value their freedom. One of the freedoms they value is who they will mate with. For a third party to say 'Here, this is your mate' is just unheard of."

Kevin rocked his eyes. "But it's done all the time on your planet. Some mates do not even meet until they are mated in a ceremony."

Gary rubbed his temples. "Okay, granted, in some cultures arranged marriages still take place but it's considered outdated by most civilized people now. But this situation does not compare to that."

"We also witness mating without ceremonies, on an almost reckless level."

"But that is of their free will."

"And other women mating for money and financial gain. They hardly chose their partners on occasions."

"Yeah, but again that's different. They chose that life. Okay, not all exactly choose it, but, well…"

Kevin waited for Gary to compose his thoughts.

"Okay," Gary continued, "Look at the women Joel brought up. They all hate him because he chose them but they did not choose him. There is just something, well, vulgar about just pointing to a woman and saying, 'Hey, you are going to sleep with me.'"

Kevin rocked some more, "We have observed that very thing many times. It usually resulted in mating taking place. Granted, not every time, but enough to make us believe that this was the proper course of action to make. They are also helping to save an entire race, our race."

Gary shook his head. "You should have just asked for volunteers, you would have gotten thousands."

"But humans do not seriously believe in extraterrestrial life. We would have exposed ourselves to human hostility and possibly the Minks if they happened to be watching this planet."

At that moment a small device that Kevin carried around with him beeped in a low, slow tone. Gary watched the completely alien symbols play across the tiny screen.

"We shall have to continue at another time and I hope we do. I still do not understand why things are okay one time, and not okay another time."

"I just, oh, it's hard to explain."

"Your ten have arrived. You took great care in your selections, Matt and Joel chose quickly. You must have very specific needs. Or do I mean tastes?"

Gary wanted to ask Kevin how Gorgons mated, but with the announcement that his ten were on board he suddenly became too nervous to think about it. The whole room seemed to spin and for a few moments nothing seemed real.

The Gorgon known as Joe came in and nodded at Kevin. Kevin nodded back and stood up. "Everything is ready." He said.

Another Gorgon walked by and Joe and Kevin stopped and stared. Gary recognized that particular Gorgon but was never told his name. He asked Kevin why all the other Gorgons stop and stare at him, something he had noticed before.

"That's Tom. Look how low he wears his ring" Kevin answered.

"Oh yeah, very low." Joe added.

Gary couldn't figure out what they were talking about but he had more important things to worry about.

20

Joel, Gary, and Matt once again stood by as 10 women were pushed in on smooth black tables. Gary wondered why he didn't think of asking to observe the changing process and was hoping he could see what happens when Matt's 10 picks were brought on board.

"Well," said Joel, "Some of these aren't so old." Matt elbowed him sharply.

"Actually," he continued, unphased by Matt's elbow, "this one is quite fetching. In fact, I'd say she's beautiful. What's her specialty?"

Matt agreed that she was quite fetching.

"Oh, her name is Amber, she worked in Washington."

The Gorgons filed out and left the three men alone.

"Good luck," said Matt, cracking a smile, "Don't let them start screaming on you." He could barely hold back a few giggles. Gary smiled and held back, too.

"Oh, you guys are real funny. We'll see how you handle it."

Matt looked again at Amber. "What does she do again?"

Gary was busy trying to match names with faces. "Oh, she worked in Washington. D.C., that is."

"Yeah, but what does she *do*?"

"Well," Gary rubbed his nose. "Actually, she's a lobbyist for the Department of Human Services."

Matt scrunched his eyebrows in thought. "A lobbyist? For DHS? Do they even have those?"

"Well, yeah."

"How is she supposed to help?"

Joel's expression went from deep thought to realization then to evil grin. "She's his backup girl." He said, nodding knowingly.

Gary shook his head. "No, she isn't."

Joel kept on grinning. "You had to have one pretty girl in case we have to go through with it. She's your backup."

"I think he's right." Said Matt, with the same grin. "What use would a lobbyist be?"

"Look…"

"Our high and mighty voice of morality has a doubt, methinks."

Gary marched up to Matt and Joel and said in a low, stern tone, "Look, I have been in love with this woman since the day we met, so please don't tell me what I'm doing. I know perfectly well what I'm doing."

"Oh, so you know her?"

Gary was starting to turn red. "Well, no, not as such."

"You never met her?" Matt couldn't believe it.

"She used to give speeches at fund raising events. And she's been on CNN a few times…"

"You never met her? I think Joel is right, she's your back up girl."

"I just thought…"

Joel, still grinning the grin that Gary wanted to punch, interrupted again. "You just thought that this was the perfect opportunity to meet the woman of your dreams. It's okay, I completely understand."

One of the women moaned.

"Just get out of here."

Joel continued, even as Gary started to push him out of the door way. "It's okay for you to do it, but if I do it I'm just a horny young man with delusions of grandeur…"

If there was more it was lost behind the door which melted down from the ceiling.

Gary pressed his fists against his eyes. He probably was doing the wrong thing but the thought that they may fail to get off the ship did occur to him. Slowly, nervously he turned back around to look at her.

Her eyes were opened.

Gary nearly jumped through the wall, it was the last thing he expected to see. Putting his hand on heart he walked forward again.

"Please, just remain calm, you are perfectly safe."

He saw more eyes and one or two women trying to sit up.

"Please, I know you are disorientated, just remain calm." He paced up and down the room using his most soothing voice he could find just reassuring and relaxing the women as much as possible. He didn't want a repeat of Joel's fiasco.

Some of the ladies began to sit up and look around but still Gary paced. He could see worry in their eyes, most notably in the eyes of Amber. Once they were all up and about he began his prepared speech.

"Ladies, I just want you all to relax and remain calm. My name is Gary and I just want to welcome you aboard the starship Tub. This is a marvelous opportunity that you've been given to be the very first humans to meet an entirely alien race."

"Wait a minute," one of the women interrupted, "Were we picked up by the same UFOs that picked up the calendar girls?"

Gary felt something worse than butterflies in his stomach. "Well, yes, actually. I wasn't aware that had made the news."

The woman continued, "Of course it made the news. UFOs. Flying saucers. I thought I saw one just like on the TV just before I passed out. Now do you care to explain just what is going on?"

"I was just getting to that. If I may continue."

The general consensus in the room was that he continue.

"You are indeed on a ship that's just outside the Earth's orbit. You have been chosen to meet with these aliens and learn about their culture."

"Except," interrupted another woman, who was slightly younger than the first, "That there are no such thing as aliens so I, for one, don't believe you."

Gary smiled. This was one argument he was certain he could win. "Oh, I assure you they are real. I've been up here for a couple of days. I've talked with them and have seen their technology. Look at these walls, do you see a crack for a door anywhere?"

While heads were turning all around the room the woman continued. "Smooth walls are not proof of an alien civilization. I was in the middle of a very busy workday and there had better be a darned good explanation for all of this."

Taking a deep breath and organizing his thoughts Gary realized the only thing to do was to show them the goods.

"Okay, in a moment I am going to open this door and behind it is Bob, the captain of this vessel. Well, not really the captain, but the defacto leader of the ship. Please don't panic and remain calm, they do have a translating device so he can talk to you and you can ask questions. Again, just stay calm."

He pointed his remote at the wall. "Just watch this, the doors here are the neatest things." The door went up revealing Bob and Joe.

Ten women caught their breath.

Bob and Joe walked into the room. Bob raised is eyes a bit and started his speech.

"Welcome aboard the starship Tub. From what I gather the translator picked a funny word for our name, but there it is."

With jaw dropped one of the ladies muttered, "They really are alien. Are you carbon based?"

"Where are you from?" Another asked.

"Is this really a ship? What propels it?"

"How are you generating gravity?"

Bob took a step backwards as questions started to bombard him.

"Do you have DNA?"

"What is this ship made out of?"

"Ladies, ladies please, I know this is all fascinating and believe me I'm still reeling from all this, but we must just stay calm and we, I mean they, will answer all your questions when we get settled in. I think the first thing we need to do is show you the window."

The women looked around with now wide eyes.

"Oh yes," said Bob, "Everybody seems to love the window."

21

Several levels down 10 now smartly dressed women watched the new arrivals on a large screen that dropped down from the ceiling for just this occasion.

"Yeah," Karen said, "Something tells me they weren't brought here for mating."

Sherri, a young brunette who was actually glad to be away from grocery store where she worked, pointed up to the screen. "Especially that one, I think the ship has sailed on her mating days."

The screen went dark and retracted back into the ceiling.

"I guess we don't get to see them look out the window."

Karen stood up. "Well, I'm starving, who wants to help me make dinner?"

Becky jumped out of her seat. "I'm a cook, what'll it be girls?"

Several holds away Matt was nudging Joel. "See? That's how it's done."

"Very funny, very funny."

Kevin also watched intently. "These women appear very different from the ones Joel chose."

Matt looked over at him. He couldn't let on what Gary was up to. "Well, we pick women for different things. Joel here is attracted to beauty, Gary is attracted to brains. It's all a matter of taste."

Joel looked over at the nearest Gorgon. "Um, Jeff, was it?"

The Gorgon looked back. "Yes, I am Jeff."

"I'm just curious, are there men and women amongst you? I mean, I'm not sure how it translates, but you all appear to be men, or male. How do you, to put it delicately, have children?"

Jeff's eyes darted around the room. The translator picked up various phrases such as "Yeah, tell them" and "Go on, don't be shy." Joel and Matt exchanged glances, this was obviously a touchy subject.

"Well," started Jeff, "When two Gorgons are at that place in life when offspring would bring them joy and the mandated forms have been filed with the agency responsible for offspring then they can retire to someplace suitably quiet and private and they, well, they…"

Kevin piped in, "I believe the human terms are make love, or mate, or fuck, or become one."

Matt and Joel had never heard a Gorgon utter a vulgar word before and both wondered if the translator knew what it was saying.

There seemed to be a general agreement around the room that this was indeed what Gorgons did.

"It's extremely pleasurable" one said.

"I'd love to do it more" another blurted out.

Matt openly laughed but tried to compose himself. A Gorgon named Benny leaned in and said, "I'm so glad we seem to find the same things humorous. You humans are all right."

"Just one of the guys." Joel flashed his smile all over the room. Then he said, "But that doesn't answer my question. Are there males and females? I hate to say it, but I can't really spot a difference between most of you."

Jeff tapped his foot nervously. "No, we are all the same. Gay? Unisex?"

"I think the translator is failing on that point. Any one of us can mate with any other of us." Said Kevin.

"Some more than others." Another Gorgon said. Matt and Joel were beginning to recognize the slight head bobs and turned eyes as laughter of sorts.

Matt said, "I think I get it. What's that word they use for flowers and plants? Bisexual? No…"

That seemed to illicit more laughter. Kevin shook his eyes, "I'm not sure if that translated correctly but we are not each two sexes. We cannot have sex with ourselves."

"Although John likes to try." One Gorgon said. Even Matt and Joel burst out laughing at that.

Joel jumped up and headed to the kitchen area. "So, what do you guys like to eat?"

The room went silent for a moment. Jeff looked around and then back at Joel, who paused at the awkward silence. "We don't absorb nutrients the same way you do. When

we need to refresh, we soak in what we need."
He looked around at the other Gorgons as if
seeking their permission to go on. Then, as if he
got it said, "Would you like to try?"

22

"Wow, it looks like someone beamed a
whole Target Superstore up here."

Ten women entered yet another hold full
of everything imaginable. Kevin had joined
Bob to help settle the women in as Joe went on
to other duties.

Kevin listened to the translator and
figured out what the woman was saying. "Oh,
no," he said, "we did experiment with matter
transference beams but in the end the power
requirements and equipment needed was so
great that it turned out to be easier to just ship
whatever it was you wanted to transfer."

"Excuse me, I'm Doctor Wei Cheng
from Rochester, I think I speak for us all when I
ask, do you have bone structure?"

Kevin look at Dr. Cheng, "Well, no
actually, it's more a fibrous support."

"And how is it possible to change a few molecules in every cell of our body?"

Bob fielded this question. "We don't know, you'll have to ask the medical technicians. They have a big machine."

Gary was getting a bit impatient. Most of the women had been doing nothing but asking questions since they woke up. There was a moment of peace when they were shown the window but that only brought a new round of even more intense questions. He was beginning to pick up on something but wasn't sure what it was exactly. He filed the feeling away for later contemplation.

In the meantime he let the women keep asking questions. He noticed one woman standing a little apart from the rest and decided it was the perfect moment to break her away from the herd.

"How are you feeling?" Gary asked.

Amber Howard shook her head and shrugged her shoulders. "This is so overwhelming. And these are such are bright women, I wonder why I'm here at all."

Gary mentally swallowed hard. "Well, I think it was just that we wanted someone from all walks of life. To get every perspective."

"We?"

Gary mentally swallowed even harder. "That will all be explained later. There's a lot going on here and it's too much to take in all at once. Can I get you anything? There's a fully stocked kitchen along that wall. It also seems to be where all the couches and chairs were arranged."

"Are there, like, quarters?"

"Um…" Gary looked over the hold. He knew what he and the boys had done but he never saw if Joel's women had made any arrangements. He was sure he saw bunk beds somewhere and they would have a remote or two to make walls. "I'll get back to you on that." Was all he managed to say.

"I would like to sit down. I feel exhausted."

"Right this way."

Kevin and Bob watched as Gary walked away from the group. "He's leaving us alone here." Muttered Bob.

Kevin gave the command to turn off the translator for a few moments and turned towards Bob. "I've got to get out of here, these females are driving me crazy."

Bob waved at him, "Turn that back on, I have an idea."

Bob looked back at the woman and pointed towards the kitchen area. "Why don't you all have a seat and Gary will explain a few things."

Nine women didn't notice the two aliens duck out the door as they headed over towards Gary.

Amber had made herself comfortable and Gary was just ready to turn on the charm and ask if he could make her anything to eat when he noticed a small crowd gathering around him.

He raised his eyebrows and looked around the group.

They all paused and stared at him.

For a moment they all stood there, waiting for something to happen.

"Yes?" Gary finally said at last.

"Bob the alien said you wanted to say something." One of the women offered.

Gary looked past the women but there was no sign of the aliens.

"Those dirty rats." He said under his breath.

23

Joel stood in front of ten calendar girls who were looking at him so intently that he put the large kitchen counter between himself and them. He was hoping things would go a little better this time.

He was hoping that having seen other women come on board they would feel a little better.

"Okay, that went much smoother."

Sherrie sat up. "I noticed he didn't say anything about mating."

Joel sighed. "He will, eventually. But you heard the story, as will they, about how the Gorgons need us. Yes, I was a jerk about it, but I'm really not thinking about myself here..."

"Oh, yes, you were." It was Karen. "You may have been picked at random but we weren't. You took a campus girls calendar, a calendar whose only purpose was to turn guys on, and used nothing but your penis to pick ten sexy girls. You know nothing about us."

Becky added, "Why didn't you at least look for women who would have jumped at this chance? I mean, I know they weren't letting you communicate, but at least that Gary guy did research. All those women are excited to be here."

Joel was feeling deflated. "Look, I was picked up by aliens, I was told I was saving a whole planet, do you really think I was thinking clearly? This is too big for me."

"So, like I said, just think with your penis. It's what men do when presented with a challenge." Karen sat back and folded her arms tensely in front of her.

Annie, whose baby was left behind looked up at him. "When is the third group coming?"

Joel just shook his head. "I don't know, tomorrow I think." He lowered his head, he really didn't know what he could say at this point.

Parminder broke the silence but was just staring off into space. "I have a husband. I love him. I want the life he was going to give me. But now I cannot go back. Why can't the aliens just bring him on board?"

Again Joel shook his head. "I don't know, they said not everyone could be changed. They said it had to be this way." He looked at the women in defeat. "I'm so sorry. I don't know what to say at this point. There's a Gorgon, I think his name is Terry, he will get you anything you need. If you can't find something tell him, they'll pick it up for you. He will come if you push this button here." He showed them a green button on one of the spare remotes that were left in the hold for their use. He pointed to the triangular green button next to it. "You know how to reach me." Sad and dejected, he left the hold.

Alicia, who had been wandering around the hold came up to the main counter and set a large box down. She held up her hand to reveal three huge diamonds on three different fingers. "I'll bet this box alone is worth millions." A few girls got up to look.

Karen rolled her eyes. "You have got to be kidding me."

"What good are riches if you cannot share them? What good are gifts that are not earned?" Parminder asked.

"Well," said Lisa, a young student, after finding a ring that was just her size and caret weight, "it takes the edge off."

***

In another part of the ship Matt sat belly deep in pit of green, sweet-smelling slime. They were chatting about the latest arrivals.

"That was not as funny as the last time." One commented. With all their sashes piled up on the floor he couldn't tell them apart. He looked at a handful of the green ooze he was sitting in.

"No, but you see, Gary hasn't brought up the mating yet. And he picked women based on intelligence rather than looks." Matt wondered what humans looked like to a Gorgon.

"Do all men have such different tastes?"

With the translator sitting on the pile of sashes it was hard to even tell who was talking.

"Well," Matt said, trying not to look at anyone in particular, "the short answer is yes, some men like legs, some like skinny women,

some don't care, some like outgoing or shy.
There's a thousand different things a man can
see in a woman."

There was a long silence.

"Humans are weird."

Matt smiled broadly and shook his head.
"Yeah, even we think that."

"Anything?"

It took Matt a moment to realize what
the question was. "Oh, sorry, no, it's relaxing
and feels okay, but I think I'll stick to human
food. Sometimes it's not what you eat, though,
it's the company that counts."

The translator said "Aww."

He wondered if should taste it but that
would be too much like drinking the water from
a Turkish bath.

The Gorgons started walking up the
ramp and stood under the dryer. They shook out
their sashes and robes and put their rear leg
rings back on. Matt had to remind himself that
these were aliens, so he shouldn't be shy about
getting out himself. Just one of the guys, he
tried to convince himself. Slowly and
cautiously he walked up the ramp and stood

under the dryer and was amazed at how the slimy goo did seem to just fall off his body.

He noticed all the Gorgons were looking at him. Shyly he said, "Well, I'd better get dressed, too."

"You're naked?"

"Um, yeah."

As he was getting dressed they continued to stare. "Your skin looks so fragile. But I hear your bones are tough." One said.

"Shouldn't they be on the outside?"

Matt wasn't sure how to even answer that. "Maybe Kevin can explain that better."

The Gorgon with the translating device walked up to Matt and said in a low voice, "Between you and us, Kevin isn't the longest rod in the coil."

Despite the odd reference, Matt understood. "Really?" he said in an equally quiet tone.

"Yes, and he's a bit of a high ringer."

Okay, Matt didn't get that one and said so.

"You know, he likes to feel important, wears his ring up high."

"Oh, do those rings indicate a rank?"

Some of the Gorgons shook their eyes.

"No, it's a sort of personal preference. He's puffing. I'm not sure how to explain it so it translates."

"I think I get it, we call someone like that a brown noser."

There was a pause then several of the Gorgons burst out in their equivalent of laughing. They started to leave the nutrient room. "Yes, I think that translated perfectly." One said.

Matt wasn't sure he knew what just happened but he smiled and walked out with them.

24

"And then our children will be able to be modified to breathe the atmosphere on the farming planet."

Ten women sat in silence in the tight circle that Gary formed. He was told he would have privacy but wasn't sure his idea of privacy was the same concept as the aliens.

He looked around then continued. "But this is not something I want to do. As you well know you were not all chosen randomly, I picked you because I thought you could help me."

"Help you what?" one of the women asked.

"I want to go home. I want to figure out what they did to me, to us, and reverse it. I want get a landing craft, and I want to head back to Earth."

After another pause Dr. Cheng leaned forward. "I have been thinking about this all night and I can't come up with a process, alien or otherwise, that could change our physiology to not need oxygen. And changed or not, one generation of offspring isn't enough for any change to propagate."

"Then again," said another woman, a Dr. Sandra Collum, physicist from the University of Illinois, "We are in orbit around the Earth. I can't begin describe how us just being here is beyond the reach of human technology at the moment. I'm fascinated by the door alone. And the window. And I, for one, would just love to be able to share this with the rest of the human race."

There was general agreement amongst the group.

A younger woman, in her late twenties waved her hand for a moment. "Captain Evlyn White, United States Air Force. Gary, did you have any sort of plan? Have these aliens shown any sort of hostility? Do they have weapons?"

Gary shook his head. "In fact, they have been overly nice to us. I get the feeling they really are treating us like heroes that are going to save them. I never thought to ask about weapons but I have been nosing around a bit in the day to day operations around here. There is a hanger with about ten of those saucers, maybe more, and also escape pods, although Bob said they have never been tested. They've never balked at answering anything I've asked them."

"Not that we know anything about the psychology of these creatures, for all we know lying could be a way of life for them." The woman looked around, then added, "Dr. Susan Hitchens, psychologist."

Captain White, who had a bit of a southern drawl, jumped in again. "Why don't we all introduce ourselves, give some background, and figure out where to go from here. And I know you're all doctors and all but my friends all call me Chase."

The introductions lasted almost an hour. There was Dr. Wei Cheng, a circulatory and blood specialist from the Mayo Clinic. Dr. Sandra Collum, a physicist, Dr. Susan Hitchens, a world-renowned psychologist, Dr. Kay Willhouse, a molecular biologist from a pharmaceutical company, Nola Blanchard, a structural engineer from MIT, Tatyana Annysherian, a computer engineer, Dr. Stephanie Axely-Young, a chemist, Dr. Katherine "Kitty" Plaitte, an astrophysicist, Captain White and finally Amber Howard, who raised some eyebrows when she introduced herself but nobody said anything.

From an enormous pile of office supplies they got some pens and notepads and started making lists and writing down questions. Not only did they want to get back to Earth, but they wanted to get back to Earth with as much technology and knowledge as they could gather.

25

Gary came in to see Matt napping in a recliner and Joel throwing a tennis ball at the back of a crate. He missed the return bounce and reached down and picked up another one from a bucket beside his chair.

"You're making a mess." Gary said simply.

Joel sighed heavily. "Yes, yes I am." As Gary plopped down in another recliner he added, "You were gone a while. Did things go well?"

"Yeah, it's amazing what's in these holds. Say, how is your group sleeping? I mean were there beds somewhere?"

"I dunno. They were all over."

"I take it things aren't going so well."

"No, they pretty much hate me."

"Well, you'll be happy to know the two you left behind are under heavy guard. It seems the flying saucers don't even try to hide themselves anymore. So much for secrecy."

"With all this Gorgon technology we can't even listen to a radio. I'm sure they'll be doing morning shows and writing books before long. They're set for life."

"It sure is quiet. I didn't see anyone on the way back here. They must observe night and day like we do. I wonder what their planet is like."

"Wet." Mumbled Matt from his slumber. "It's wet and slimy. But their sky is still blue."

"Oh?"

"I went and absorbed nutrients," he said using air quotes, "with them. They are so, well, alien, but at the same time they're just like us. And don't ask me how I know, but they can't tell when we're naked."

Gary smiled a little. "You know, it doesn't matter if we go with them, if we make it back to Earth we're set for life, too."

Joel idly picked up another tennis ball, "Or locked up in the loony bin."

"You know, they didn't mention if we were in the news. I wonder if any of us have been linked with the UFOs yet. I mean, I think they were more secret about us."

"A couple of missing persons is nothing compared to UFOs kidnapping models and scientists."

Gary watched a tennis ball roll past his feet. "I wonder what's going on down there." He flipped open the notebook he brought back with him.

Joel glanced up, "What's that?"

"A list of equipment I'm going to ask for. Did either of you find anything missing that you wanted? Joe said they could get anything."

"Diapers." Was all Matt said.

Joel threw another ball. "Nope, no chance I'll be needing those."

26

The three men stood together waiting for the last group to arrive.

"You ready for this, big guy?" said Gary.

"I think I am. Avoid screaming, keep them calm. Check."

Joel squinted his eyes, "Yeah, very funny."

"Did you get your doctors in to see the transformation?"

Gary glanced down the hallway. "Yes, I hope they learn something. Of all the things going on that seems to be the most unbelievable to them. I heard one of the Gorgons talking, it seems there was a little problem this time. Not sure what happened but they said something about meeting some resistance and somebody got hurt."

"One of the girls?"

"No, a Gorgon."

Just then the ladies arrived on their black tables pushed by ten Gorgons.

Joel's eyes widened just a little. "Dude."

Even Gary was a little taken aback. "Um, okay." Then added, after the last table came through, "Whoa. That's a baby."

Indeed, on the last table was a small baby. Joel shook his head when he realized who it was. "Way cool, Matt."

As the Gorgons filed out Gary tried to stop one of them but realized that none had a translator. Remembering the instructions from Kevin he pushed the appropriate button on his remote and spoke into it. "Wait, can you tell me if anything happened on this trip?"

It took a moment as the remote seemed to not work nearly as well as the regular ones. "Toby…hit with…projectiles…uncoiled. In…medical…recoiling."

"Will he be alright?"

"Yes…no…harm."

"I sure hope so. Thanks."

"No…problemo."

Gary turned back and looked at the baby. "We should find some blankets."

Joel couldn't hold it in any longer. "So, Matt, you like fat chicks or what?"

Taking a deep breath, Matt leaned over one of the women. "This is Melody. She's my fiancé. I couldn't spend the rest of my life without her. But, well, you know, I didn't want her to think I was taking advantage of the situation so I decided I would just make sure all the other women I picked weren't as attractive as she was. So she knows it's about helping the Gorgons and not about sex. This is going to be hard enough to explain, I didn't want nine hotties complicating things. And when I saw that woman so hysterical about her baby I talked with Bob about her being one of mine, after all, it is a girl but she'll grow up and bear children as far as the Gorgons are concerned."

Joel was looking at one woman in particular. "Backup chick?" Gary threw him a dirty look.

"No." said Matt. "That's Kim, Melody's sister. I figured I would make this as easy as I could for Melody so brought her along so Melody would have someone to relate to."

Gary and Joel exchanged glances. "Dude, you brought your fiancé's sister? You didn't see the flaw in that plan?"

Matt admitted he didn't.

Joel tried to be diplomatic. "Okay, so you love your bride to be. She's cute but no offense, has a few extra pounds on her. Nothing wrong with that. But her sister is hot, and you bring her, too. Don't you think she'll question that?"

Matt shook his head.

"She's going to totally think you have a thing for her sister and that now you took advantage of the whole Gorgon soap opera to act on it."

"No, no, no." Matt said, smiling. "She would never think that. It's all about family, that I did a nice thing for her."

"Matt," said Gary as he turned to leave. "Take my advice. Never tell any of these women you picked them because they were unattractive to you."

"Unless you want a riot on your hands. Anyway, I'm going to go tell what's her name that her baby is safe."

"You don't even know their names yet?" Gary said as they walked out the door together. It silently slid to the floor leaving Matt alone and nervous with nine very large women.

***

John watched on his view screen as Matt calmed nine women down and kept wrapping his arms around one of them. He wondered what weird alien behavior this was and tried to figure out why that one was so special. Maybe she was a leader of some kind.

There was a gong at the door and he invited Kevin in.

"That is the last of them. We will do a few more supply runs and then all stores shall be complete. It looks as if there were many things we didn't think of but the women have given us lists. We will give this lot a chance to give us a list as well."

"Why was one brought that was so young?"

"It was a compromise. It is the offspring of one of the first lot. It will bring peace to that group and it is a female after all so he will still mate with it. Also, two of the second group wanted to see the molecular chamber. I told Evan not to show them too much."

John bobbed his eyes up and down. "A compromise?" He didn't expect a response. "They aren't staying where they are supposed to stay, they aren't happy with what we brought them, they don't seem to want to cooperate with anyone. They are using water at a greater rate that we previously thought. I wonder what else they will do."

Kevin was once again a bit insulted. He, above all else, knew that humans were unpredictable and John should realize this. He suspected that John did realize this and was just making a point of making sure everyone knew about it.

"We will be leaving in a few days. All the programs are set."

"At least we know what we're doing." John gave the command to open the window. "I wonder how humans got so far. It's one thing to survive in all the climates and conditions that are down there, but they just seem too scatterbrained to develop technology." He turned abruptly to Kevin. "Keep me informed."

Without another word Kevin turned and left.

***

"You don't hold a baby like that." Marissa, a data entry clerk at an insurance company, laid a blanket out on the table and put the baby on it then wrapped it up nice and tight like a little burrito. She then cradled it in her arms and rocked it a little and for the first time since it woke up it stopped crying.

Joel thanked her. "You'd better get going, you don't want to miss the window. Then I'm sure Bob and Kevin will want to talk with you all in your store room. I'll take this little one to her mother."

"Can't I see the window later?" She smiled. "Show me the back stage stuff."

Marissa handed the baby over to Joel but it started crying as soon as she let go. He immediately gave it back to her which it acknowledged by not crying once again.

Joel nodded. "Sure, come with me." They both smiled this time.

As they turned to leave an unidentifiable Gorgon passed the door and idly looked at them as it passed.

Marissa took a deep breath. "Are you sure they are safe?"

"About as safe as I am."

She giggled. "Are you sure they are safe?" she asked again.

"Ha, ha." Joel said flatly, and they headed off towards the calendar girls' hold.

***

Annie, who had been watching along with the other girls, paced back and forth near the entrance to the hold. Another woman was trying to keep her calm.

"Okay, was it just me or were those the biggest women you ever saw?" Lisa was saying.

Karen rolled her eyes. She had been tracing her scars the whole time she watched this batch wake up. "None of us are perfect."

"Oh, come on. We were picked for our beauty, Gary pick brains, what do you think they are? Brawn? Remind me never to date a farmer."

Becky put her hand on Karen's arm. "Let it go."

"Nobody should be judged on how they look." Karen made it a point to say this loud enough for Lisa to hear.

"I know." Becky didn't care if Lisa heard or not. "And no one should be judged in this situation at all. We're all under stress here."

Lisa, Karen, Becky and the others watched as Joel and Marissa walked in and at the tearful reunion that followed.

"Look," said Joel, "I really didn't know…"

"Just don't talk to me." Was all Annie could say to him.

Parminder, who was sitting on her own caught his eye. "I wish my husband were here." Joel heaved a sigh and turned to leave.

Marissa glanced around and headed out after him. "It was nice meeting you all." Was all she could think of saying.

After the door went down she told Joel how she thought they were being harsh on him.

"Don't they know that this is the biggest thing ever and we're all a part of it?"

"Maybe you can explain that to them."

"When the news broke that first a bunch of models, and then a bunch of scientists all got picked up by UFOs, who would've thought they'd pick someone like me? It's like hitting the jackpot."

"What do you mean, someone like you?"

"Well, I'm not exactly a model, and I'm no scientist. I barely make more than minimum wage. Why would aliens care about me?"

Joel had been pressing the door button as he walked, he couldn't figure out how Gorgons knew where the doors were. One finally opened and he could hear Bob through a translator. "I'd better let you get back to your group. You don't want to miss any of this."

He was relieved he wouldn't have to answer her last question.

***

Hours later Joel was neatly stacking strips of bacon on wheat as if weaving some sort of meat cloth into a work of art.

Gary watched, almost fascinated, as he ate a tasty cantaloupe.

"I found that if I kept the griddle slightly tilted the grease ran off quicker and the bacon comes out crispier." It seemed as if Joel was just talking to himself. "Then I can layer the sandwich and my bites are cleaner, some mayo on top and ketchup on the bottom…"

At that moment Matt and Bob walked in and stood by the counter. They didn't say anything as they watched Joel put the finishing touches on his sandwich and take a big bite.

"Hmmm, maybe I should toast the bread and melt a slice of cheese on top."

Bob stared for a moment then said, "It's just like us, only inside out. We absorb through our outer skin nutrients that are all ready for absorbing but you have to process the raw material and then absorb it on the inside. It's like your whole body does everything on the inside."

Gary nodded, that about summed it up.

Bob continued with his observations. "Since your skin doesn't really do anything except hold you together it's almost independent of the environment. Hot, cold, wet, dry, it doesn't matter because all the processing takes place on the inside."

Joel paused his eating. "Add protective clothing and we can do even more." He took another bite.

Matt took a deep breath. "Well, as fascinating as this all is, we need to talk. Now that everyone is on board we were thinking of getting them all together so we can all get to know each other."

Gary chuckled. "A mixer."

"Then after, we'll have a big meeting and see if there's anything else we need to bring on board. And how much of everything we may need."

"We can leave you alone if you wish but there are still many on board that haven't met you humans yet and they are just as curious as you all are."

"I think the Gorgons would be more than welcomed." Nodded Gary. "What would a mixer be without our honored hosts?"

Then Gary turned more serious. "What exactly happened down there? I understand someone got hurt."

Bob gathered his thoughts. "Well, as you know we wanted to remain a secret but some of our equipment malfunctioned so we just decided to go for it. After the mother was taken, the baby was taken to a building where there were guards and many people about. It was almost as if they were expecting us. Since they couldn't wait for the infant to come out they had to leave their ship and enter the building. We have equipment that we were told would deflect the type of bullets humans use but it didn't seem to hold up. We don't always get a choice on who builds these things for us, you see."

"Was he hurt?"

"You mean Toby? Well, we are made primarily of fibrous bundles and each bundle, whether it is an originating strand or primary function bundle, is fully independent and expendable. We don't bleed, or have blood, or feel pain the same way that you do. It was merely an inconvenience to him. Once he regenerates he will be just like before. Oh, except for maybe a little white spot, until it wears in."

Gary thought about something the pilot said. "Bob," he started carefully, "this may be an uncomfortable question, but just out of curiosity, what would it take to kill one of you?"

Even Joel froze up a little but Bob didn't seem to mind.

"Well, our thought center, or what you would call a brain I think, is in a primary bundle down the center of our mass. As long as that remains intact we can rejuvenate our whole body if need be from there, although the eyes are a bit tricky. You'd have to hack us down to that, and then destroy that. The thought center can live on its own without a body since it is a fibrous bundle on its own, it would just need to find some nutrients to soak in like any other body."

"Wow."

Matt was listening quietly. "That makes our own bodies sound so complicated. We have blood and organs and bones, any one of which can kill us if injured."

Bob thought it would be best not to mention how fragile he thought they all were and how many humans were broken in finding that out. Not to mention how many were broken in the abduction of the baby. And a few in the gathering of the tremendous amount of merchandise in all the holds. He wasn't sure how they would react to such news.

After a long silence, Matt looked at his watch. "Let's say 24 hours from now. That will give my bunch a chance to get settled in and rested and we'll open up a neutral hold. Everybody bring a dish."

They all generally agreed that this sounded like a plan.

***

In another part of the ship Melody and Kim sat alone on a couch and watched the other women mill about finding places to rest for the night.

"I know he didn't volunteer for this, and that he didn't have a choice once he was up here, but look who he picked."

Kim nodded but didn't say anything.

Melody continued. "Why do you think he picked those women? Am I like that? Why didn't he pick pretty women? Is that how he sees me?"

Kim shook her head. "You are way more attractive than those women. I don't know what his problem is."

Melody rested her head on the couch. "I never felt so ugly in my life."

***

Thirty feet down a completely different conversation was taking place. Dr. Cheng was voicing her frustrations at what she was able to witness when the last group of women were brought on board.

"They just wheeled the women in, lowered a wall, pushed a few buttons, then raised the wall up again. I didn't get see any instrumentation, or processes, or anything."

"Yes," added Dr. Willhouse, "the Gorgon operating the controls didn't seem to have the slightest idea what was happening. He just said it was proprietary and the programmers would decoil him if he gave out any secrets. I even asked if I could go through it again and he said it'd never been done that way."

"I didn't get anywhere either, if it's any consolation." Said Nola Blanchard, the structural engineer. "I questioned a Gorgon named Lenny at length about the artificial gravity and apparently there are a few methods in which it can be achieved. When the ship was built one method was chosen over another by some sort of lottery or bidding process, he wasn't sure which, and since the makers of artificial gravity are in fierce competition it's all guarded industrial secrets. All he could tell me was that you push a button to turn it on, and you push another to turn it off. Oh, and that the actual equipment is in a part of the ship where no one goes."

"I would kill to know how to make artificial gravity." She added.

"Yeah, I suppose they'll say the same thing about faster than light travel as well."

Nola nodded. "I asked him about that, too. He just said it was complicated."

"Oh, this is stupid, we're getting nowhere."

They all stared at their own little worlds for a few moments. Dr. Willhouse broke the silence. "At least I learned a little about them, as a species. They seem to be plant based, or at least closer to plants as we know them than animals. I know this sounds strange but as fluid as they are they seem to have no moving parts. I can't wait to get one under a microscope."

The women launched into a technical discussion on theories of how things worked with amazed statements that things worked at all. Feeling alone and outside of all the conversations sat Amber, wondering what her roll would be and if she could live up to it when the time came.

27

Karen had gotten up, showered, and was poking around the kitchen area thinking that life aboard an alien spacecraft hovering over the Earth was actually quite boring. She had no idea what time it was, she just felt it ought to be early morning and that she would like some eggs. Even though she was being rather quiet and enjoying her alone time she welcomed the sight of Becky, in a brand new, comfortable looking sweat suit, wearily walking up to the counter.

"Eggs?"

"Sure." Becky sat on stool and felt as if she was in a large, surreal diner. "Sunny side up?"

"Sure. I don't suppose we have any way of making toast."

Becky shrugged her shoulders. "I'm sure we do, but I'm too tired to walk the miles of aisles we have here."

Karen turned the burner on and had to wait a moment or two to see where the counter was getting hot before she put her skillet down. Becky, feeling just a little guilty that she wasn't helping decided to find something to drink.

"Milk or juice?" she asked, opening the door to one of the refrigerated areas. As she came out she was only mildly surprised to see Parminder seating herself at the counter.

"Egg?" Karen offered.

"No, just juice will be fine, thank-you."
Parminder stared at one of the remote controls
that was setting on the counter. Somebody had
written 'Terry' under one button and 'Joel'
under another.

For a few moments the crackling of eggs
and clinking of dishes were the only sounds in
the hold,

Becky put her hand on Parminder's
shoulder. "Are you okay? I know this isn't
easy."

Parminder shook her head. "I have been
kidnapped. And even so, my husband is very
traditional, if Joel touches me he will have
nothing to do with me ever."

"Oh, don't worry," said Karen, sliding
some eggs onto a plate, "Joel won't be touching
any of us."

Parminder picked up the remote and idly
ran her thumb over the button marked Terry.

"What are you thinking?"

"Do you think he would come this
early?"

Becky shook her head. "We don't even know if they sleep. What are you thinking, sweetie?"

Taking a deep breath, she pushed the button. "I just want to know for sure."

Karen walked around and gave Parminder a one armed hug, with the other she put a plate of eggs in front of Becky. "We are behind you all the way. You're not alone."

"Yeah," said Becky, giving her a good hearted nudge. "Besides, didn't you hear? We're all famous now. The calendar ten, or something. Your husband knows that whatever happens, it's not your fault."

The door went up so quietly that if they hadn't been facing it, the girls would have never known it went up at all. Terry took a few steps in, looked around, then took a few more. To the three at the counter it looked very much like he was nervous.

"Did somebody need something?" he said quietly through the box on his back.

Parminder, who was suddenly very nervous herself, raised her hand slightly. Terry walked up to her and two completely different life forms tried in their own ways to calm themselves.

"Anything at all." Terry said.

"I want to know…" Parminder started, then took a deep breath, "I mean, I want to go home, I don't want to be here and I don't want to take part in this."

Becky and Karen exchanged glances. It was a very polite request made in all sincerity, they weren't sure how Terry would respond.

Terry's whole body drooped just enough to barely be noticeable. "I am so sorry," he said calmly and quietly, "but that is not possible. If it were up to me I would take you home immediately, but you wouldn't last two minutes in your own atmosphere. I'm afraid these things have taken place, and we cannot take you back."

Without hesitation Parminder replied. "Then two minutes in my husbands arms. That is all I ask. I would rather die there than to live here."

Terry's eyes dropped a few inches. Only another Gorgon would recognize this as crying, and Terry didn't realize that the tears running down Karen and Becky's faces were also crying. "I am so, so sorry but that is beyond the power of any of us. I will tell Bob, but I do not think that even he would deviate from orders, and he certainly would not want any harm to come to any of you. I really am so sorry."

Parminder, never once losing her composer, very politely said, "Thank-you, Terry."

"If there is anything else I can do for you, please, do not hesitate to call me. Anytime, for any reason."

He stood there for a moment as Parminder just nodded and looked away. Sensing there was nothing else he took a few steps backwards then turned around and slowly left. The door silently slid to the floor.

"Well," said Parminder, "There was no harm in asking."

"Did I miss something?"

Only slightly startled the three turned around to see Cindi, an exotic blond in a silk chamois and several carats worth of diamonds spread across her fingers, walking up to the counter.

Becky shrugged her shoulders. "Par just wanted to ask if she could go home and of course Terry said no. Nothing big."

"Egg?"

"No, actually, I just wondered if any of you were using this." She picked up the remote from in front of Parminder. "I really wanted to see the stars again, and the Earth. It's so beautiful just floating out there. Anyone want to come?"

They all declined and Cindi pointed the remote at the door and pushed the appropriate button and with a smile walked out like a princess in a castle.

After a few moments of staring at the open door Karen rolled her eyes and said, "What's the matter? Was she born in a barn?"

***

At that moment Tracy, an office supply rep, was already staring at the little blue ball hanging in space in front of her. It was mesmerizing. Her thoughts kept jumping between worrying about who was going to take over her accounts to realizing that she never had to worry about her accounts again and how she was going to pay the rent to realizing she would never have to pay rent again. The whole situation was so much to wrap her mind around.

She had never really thought about aliens before, they belonged in the same category as bigfoot and ghosts – something she just never really believed in. She wondered where god was in all of this and if the aliens had a Jesus of their own appear on their planet.

Her thoughts were interrupted by a heavy sigh.

"I'm sorry, I didn't hear you come in." Tracy thought the young girl looked remarkably underdressed.

"No problem, I just didn't think anyone would be up this early. Just wanted to enjoy the view." She walked up to the invisible wall and leaned against it. She could actually see a tiny sun reflected off a tiny ocean. "Damn, isn't that gorgeous?"

Tracy agreed that it was gorgeous. "You must be one of the first two groups."

"THE first group." Cindi said in a voice that made Tracy suddenly want to slap her.

But keeping things civil she just said, "Oh, one of the calendar girls."

"Cindi"

"Well, they never really mentioned you guys by name. Unless you looked it up of course. You can't escape the pictures, though, they are everywhere."

"Really?" Cindi smiled. Without turning around she asked, "So why were you guys brought up?"

"What do you mean?"

"I mean," said Cindi, without ever turning around, "We were picked because we're models, then the scientists, then, well, you guys. It doesn't really make sense."

Tracy's jaw dropped a little. "We're just that Matt guy's pick is all. You'll have to ask him. Weren't you just Joel's picks?"

"I guess. Still, we do all seemed to be grouped."

Tracy knew what she was getting at. The whole world knew that ten models, then ten scientists had been picked up by UFOs, then ten more, what? Losers? It wasn't lost on any of Matt's group that they were all kinda large, had menial jobs, and didn't seem to be UFO-worthy. She had accepted Matt's explanation that it was all random for him, and that Joel was a jerk who just picked a random calendar, and that Gary was attracted to brains but she really didn't like that Cindi was picking up on what the press was saying about the first two groups and what they might be saying about the third.

But rather than start anything she just stood up and said, "Well, I guess I'll go see if anyone is up yet. Enjoy the view."

Cindi didn't say anything as Tracy left.

***

Five minutes later Tracy walked back into her hold and was surprised to see everyone gathered around the counter laughing and talking. Matt and Melody seemed to be entertaining the troops. A few of the girls noticed her and waved her over.

Matt looked up and said, "Hey…"

"Tracy"

"Hey, Tracy. Pull up a stool." Then added, "Is something wrong?"

Tracy rolled her eyes. "I just met one of the models. Stuck up bitch. I just wanted to throw her out the window."

A general "oohhh" went around the counter.

"She seemed like she was better than us just because she was here first or something."

Matt just shook his head. "Oh, well, Joel wasn't quite using his brain when he was asked to pick. What'll it be? I'm making pancakes and we found all kinds of toppings."

Tracy sat down. "For some reason, I'm craving an egg."

***

Kevin and Terry found Joel sitting in front of the window, literally staring into space.

"We've been looking all over for you."

"Oh? What can I do for you?" He kept staring out the window.

Terry took a few steps forward. "I'm a little worried about Parminder. She seems very upset, even more so than the rest."

"Who?"

"She's a member of your group. Haven't you learned their names yet?"

Joel shrugged, "It's not like they'll let me hang out with them or anything."

"Which brings me to my next point. We are really counting on this mission to work. The lives of my species depends on it. We will be leaving for Halfway in a few days, we want to be sure you can work things out."

"Halfway?"

"I'm not sure how that translated, but that is the name we've given the planet you are going to colonize."

"I like it. Halfway." Joel mulled the meaning over in his mind.

"Joel…" Kevin said.

"Oh, don't worry, I'll smooth things over. Somehow." Doesn't mean there'll be any mating he added in his head.

"I was just going to say that Gary said he had a psychologist with him. He suggested that you talk to her. He said…"

"It's okay, really."

"Well, okay then. We'll leave it up to you. We'd just thought we'd mention it."

"We'll be off then." Said Terry. "Kevin are I are going to a special soak."

"Oh, really? What kind of special soak?"

"Oh, um…"

"Er…"

The Gorgon's hesitation caused Joel to turn around for the first time. He squinted his eyes and asked them again.

"Well," said Terry, "Kevin asked me out. The whole ship was given some time off and many of us are taking the opportunity to, uh…"

Kevin broke in. "To have some recreation. To relax a little."

Joel smiled and nodded his head. "It's a date. Aren't you two, um, cute? Together, that is."

Both aliens lowered their eyestalks just slightly. Joel got the distinct impression that this was equivalent to blushing. "I thought there was paperwork or something involved."

Terry and Kevin exchanged glances. Kevin tapped a foot on the floor and said, "Well, we are light years from home, totally isolated. We sort of expect to bend the rules a little bit and with some time off many of us may, as you say, date…"

"Oh, please," Joel interrupted, "you don't have to explain anything to me, I know how it is. I don't think there is a human alive who doesn't break the rules completely. It's what makes us human. I think it's great you guys can cut loose a little bit. Really."

Both Gorgon's eyestalks straightened out. "Alright, we'll be going, but please, keep an eye on Parminder. And don't forget about your party. Or mixer, or whatever it's called. We all plan to be there."

"Okay, you two have fun. Don't do anything I wouldn't do."

What appeared to be a chuckle came out of the translator. "Since it's physically impossible for you to do what we are planning, I'm afraid we'll have ignore your advice."

Joel smiled even bigger. "You go, girl."

Before Kevin could start another discussion about the gender of Gorgons Terry led him out of the room. The door slid shut and Joel turned back towards the stars, trying to guess which girl was Parminder.

***

Joel decided to wander back to the hold and make some dinner. He wondered what his group was up to and if he should check in on them. With Matt's fiancé here and Gary spending time with his group Joel found that he was a bit lonely.

"Hello, Joel." Said two Gorgons coming from the other direction.

"Hello...you." Smiled Joel. He thought he must really take more of an effort to learn names, or even how to tell them apart.

He passed an opened door and glanced inside. It was another warehouse, full of boxes as far as he could see, only this one didn't have a living or kitchen area towards the front. Without thinking he wandered in and started reading labels. It took a moment or two to realize that someone was already inside.

The sound was so distant that Joel wasn't sure he heard it at first but it persisted so he walked towards it.

"Hello." He called. The sound stopped. For some reason this really unnerved him and memories of horror movies suddenly filled his senses with the realization that he was alone in a warehouse on board an alien ship. It was always the wise ass that was eaten first.

Joel started to slowly back towards the door when a familiar voice answered back. "Hello? Is someone there?" it said.

It was Marisa.

Letting out a sigh of relief he put on a smile and walked towards her. Before he realized what was happening she raised a gun a pulled the trigger.

                    ***

Joe the Gorgon sat on a stool by two other Gorgons and stayed totally enthralled by the conversation he was having. Humans seemed impressed by his level of knowledge, which was average for a Gorgon, and he felt quite elated at the attention this was garnering him.

"Well, we have found nine planets with life," he was saying, "and several more that contain everything necessary to sustain life. Only two have had any kind of intelligence and one of them is you. So the theory is really untestable yet, but so far it seems to be true."

Nola, whose architectural skills were known as cutting edge, was only a bit disappointed in what she was learning. "So, all three civilized planets built at right angles? Our houses really look like yours?"

"Oh, yes. I can't speak for the Minks, of course, nobody has seen their planet up close, but four walls is the simplest design and a slanted roof diverts precipitation, rectangular doors still are the easiest to construct and hinge and windows are still needed to let in light and offer a view of what's outside. I will admit the more complex and stylized houses are a bit different from yours, but I think it's still along the same design principles. Structures always maintain a function first, then it's just decorated to taste."

"And is black to taste? I notice almost all the surfaces here are black."

"Well, everything here is constructed of a plasticized polymer that we can mold into just any shape we like, it just happens to be black and attempts to colorize it prohibit it's shape changing ability so we live with black."

"Shape changing plasticized polymer?"

"Oh yes, very versatile and rugged. Perfect for making ships out of."

Even though this was out of their fields of study the other women and Gary sat mesmerized by the conversation.

"And only nine planets with life? Out of how many?"

"Oh, thousands. Uncountable. Some life was only microbial, mind you, but others had developed complex ecosystems."

"Did life develop independently then?" asked Dr. Willhouse.

"We think so. There are some planets out there that seem to be perfect for life. Liquid oceans, rich atmospheres, moderate temperatures, but no life at all. And I'm no biologist but I'm told the chemical composition of each planet with life is vastly different so it supposes that life developed independently."

"This ought to knock the creationists right on their ears." Dr. Collum said.

"Creationists?"

"Do Gorgons have religion? Do you have a god?" Dr. Collum asked.

Joe pondered for a moment. "If that translated correctly, then yes, we have religion. It's not something many of us believe in but some do believe that there is a universal consciousness that we all return to after death and that it can sometimes influence the events that we find ourselves part of, if you talk to it hard enough. Tom is a believer, you should consult with him if you'd like to know more."

"Would I. I'd love to see how your gods compare to our gods."

"I think the main difference is, as much as I know, is that we have one and you seem to have many. And from what Kevin has told me you let your gods actually rule you and tell you what to do whereas we only pay homage to ours."

"Wise. Our gods have cause more and bloodier wars than anything else on the planet."

Almost everyone nodded while contemplating this statement.

"From what I understand, not only do you have political boundaries but you also have religious boundaries that overlap. I tried to follow the seminars but it all was so confusing." Joe was starting to get out of his comfort zone.

"Well," said Dr. Hitchens, "It's a good thing you picked us all up from the same country or you might have had little wars right here on your ship."

"Assuming everything works as planned we were going to pick groups from each nation. At least I think that was the plan. Bob is in charge of that."

"Do you have political boundaries?"

"We have a few, but they are not as severely divided as yours. Ours mostly exists because of physical boundaries on the planet. Before the days of mass communication it was hard to govern across mountains and oceans. What exists today is mainly a throwback to those times."

"This is so fascinating. You know, back on Earth I'd be famous for talking with the first aliens to visit our planet."

Joe twisted his eyes slightly. "Well, you know, this is special for us, too. The crew of Tub were all chosen by a committee made up of representatives from all our governments. This is our first peaceful contact and the matter of saving our race is monumental. We will all enjoy celebrity when we return to our planet."

Dr. Hitchens' face dropped. "We won't be able to enjoy the same. It's a pity."

After an awkward pause they continued to compare various world governments, each species fascinated with the similarities more than the differences.

***

Joel crouched down between two pallets of copy paper and could see four eyes bobbing down the next aisle. He rocked his gun from side to side to make sure it had a full load and then, with a burst of adrenaline jumped up and fired at the surprised Gorgon.

The Gorgon fired back with not one, but two of the exact same guns soaking Joel from his neck to his knees. Marisa, who was waiting for the right moment, popped up from behind some boxes and soaked Joel's back.

Joel cried out and dropped to his knees. "You got me!" The Gorgon's eyes bobbed uncontrollably and Marisa double over with laughter.

Joel, too, started laughing. "Wow, these holds are perfect for this."

"We should get some paintballs" Said Marissa, still giggling and sitting on the edge of a pallet.

"Oh, too messy, at least water evaporates." Joel was pulling his shirt away from his skin, trying to move a little air through the fabric to dry it off, but failing.

"This is exhilarating. I haven't played this hard in a long time." Said the Gorgon.

"And you are good at it. Your little trick worked perfectly."

"I knew you two were in cahoots."

"It's the oldest trick in the book" the gorgon said, putting his water blasters on some boxes. "I hate to leave you, but I was supposed to relieve Carl a while ago. We simply must do this again with more people."

"That would be great." Marissa fired one last shot at the Gorgon as he headed towards the exit. Then she turned towards Joel, and laughed at him holding his shirt away from his chest.

"Who would've thought that aliens just like to have to fun? Just like us." She said, then added, "What was his name again?"

"Actually, I have no idea. I only know a few by sight. They are pretty laid back if you ask me. They may look like big piles of string but they act just like the night crew in a Walmart or something. They can be funny, too."

"Speaking of Walmart, you know I'm sitting on a big box of generic t-shirts. Would you like a dry one?"

"Every single time I turn around I find something I need. It's amazing."

Marissa pulled the top off and started digging through the pile. "No four X's. They obviously weren't expecting me."

"Come on, you look fine." Joel picked a shirt and was only a little shy about exposing his body in front of Marissa.

"I'll take that compliment," she grinned, "coming from the guy who picked ten models."

Joel shook his head. "I'll never live that down. What are you laughing at?"

"Nothing. Just looks like you peed your pants is all."

They were silent for a few awkward moments then Marissa said, "Let's go explore."

Joel shrugged his shoulders. "I've seen just about everything in these holds."

"No, I mean the rest of the ship. What's further down the hallway? What's up? What's down?"

"I really don't know if we should, or even if we could."

"Oh, come on, live a little. What's the worse that can happen? We get kicked out of the engine room? I can live with that. You said yourself these guys are pretty laid back."

Joel thought for a moment. "Okay, if you can find me dry pants, I'll go."

Marissa smiled. "Will sweats do?"

28

Dr. Hitchens looked around the hold and nodded her head. "That should be enough room, I would think. We should put some more tables out, it's not like there will be dancing or anything."

Matt and Melody agreed and went off in search of something appropriate, leaving Dr. Hitchens alone with the two Gorgons who came to help set up for the mixer.

"How do you guys throw a party?"

"Well," said Joe, feeling a little uncomfortable as this was out of his element, "We usually have more a purpose. It just seems, um, different to us to have a gathering simply for the sake of meeting others. We may do that if, say, a bunch of gardeners wanted to gather to discuss gardening, but not so much to just meet each other because they had gardening in common."

"Interesting. Do you celebrate birthdays or anything?"

"No. We do celebrate births, and perhaps special breakthroughs or such, but not annually as I understand you do."

"But surely you have a social life."

Joe pondered the translation for a moment. "Well, we do, but it's not as formalized as this. We meet in the course of our day to day lives, not at what you would call social gatherings."

"You don't mind that we will be eating, do you?"

"Oh, not at all. If you don't mind my saying, we feel that it's odd to eat when it's not needed, something humans seem to do all the time."

"Sometimes it's just an icebreaker."

"Icebreaker?"

"Oh. Well, an icebreaker is something that starts a conversation between two people so they have something common to talk about at first, so that they can catch a glimpse of the other's personality. It sets a sort of baseline."

"I see. We do that, too. I just wasn't sure that translated correctly. For a moment I thought I would have freeze some water."

Dr. Hitchens thought for a moment, she wasn't really sure how the expression came about. Before she could gather her thoughts Matt and Melody returned with two card tables.

"Those look strangely out of place here." She said.

The other Gorgon spoke for the first time. "Why don't we just do this?" He pulled out his remote, which looked more complicated than the ones given to the humans and pressed a few buttons. Two flat-topped tables rose out of the floor.

Melody looked around. "Can you do that anywhere? I think they would go better over here."

"Sure. We can make some stools as well. And we'd better add some walls, I'm not sure how humans feel but we like little walls to talk over"

For the next thirty minutes or so the humans and Gorgons set up the perfect party area and almost forgot completely that this would be the very first human-Gorgon social event in all of history.

***

Joel had an uneasy feeling deep in the pit of his stomach that he couldn't quite put his finger on. There was just something about Marisa and the way she could get him to do things that he really didn't feel comfortable doing.

"I can't get this remote to do anything. Maybe it's broken." Marisa shook the small black device and then hit it with the heel of her hand a few times.

"It's not a flash light." Joel smiled.

"Actually, it is." Marisa pushed a button with her thumb and a bright bream of light shot out from the device.

Joel stared in amazement.

"Do you mean to tell me," Marisa said, noting the look on his face, "That you've been here longer than me, was shown how to use this, and you didn't know it could be a flashlight?"

"I just thought it could translate and open doors and stuff. I didn't try every button. What if I activated an airlock or something?"

They both smiled and paused, as they were at another intersection. It looked exactly like the other twenty intersections they had gone through. "I'm totally lost."

Straight ahead was a T-intersection which was only slightly different than the 4 way intersections they had been getting lost in so they decided to head that way. They weren't disappointed.

"Pipes."

Joel nodded. "Yes, pipes."

Lining the walls in either direction were large pipes, about six to a wall, and capped with hinged caps. There were little lights and buttons on the wall in front of each pipe but no two were the same. Some blinked red, some had steady amber, and others had combinations of different colors. Towards the end of one hall they thought they spotted some stars and indeed it was a round window, about four feet across.

"Finally." Marisa said, heading towards the window.

At the end of the hall the pipes had smooth rounded ends but one looked almost transparent. Joel tried to peer inside but it was only darkness.

For a long moment they stared at the stars. This view was different as there was no Earth or moon and no sun. Just points of light in utter blackness.

"Look! Orion. I guess it didn't occur to me that we could see constellations out here but I guess it makes sense. But there are so many more stars than I've ever seen in Orion. It's gorgeous."

Joel nodded. For a moment he forget everything and stared at the beauty before him.

A sudden clang made them both jump and Joel turned just in time to see a Gorgon go around the corner. The sudden feeling that they might be in a part of the ship they weren't supposed to be in washed over him along with a strange feeling that he was on ship full of aliens and anything was possible, even a mean alien discovering humans alone in the dark.

He shook his head. So far all he had met were entirely nice Gorgons, the thought of a mean one didn't fit at all. Still he told Marisa they should find their way back somehow.

"Yeah." She said, idly tapping a pipe as they started to leave. It rang very slightly.

Joel rapped another one with his knuckle and it rang a little more. As they walked towards the intersection they tapped out an impromptu rhythm, smiling at how in synch they were.

Just a few steps away one of the little doors swung open with a clang causing Joel and Marisa to jump back, hearts pounding. An eye slowly floated out of the end and curled around to look directly at them.

Marisa choked back a scream but Joel had already let one out. The eye bobbed a few times and stretched out further, followed by a mouth. It took a few moments for them to realize the mouth was moving. Coming to his senses Joel raised the remote, which was causing his hand to shake tremendously, and pressed the translation button.

"H-hello." He stammered.

"Do you mind?" The mouth said through the jerky sounding translator. "I am trying to sleep."

Joel's mouth moved up and down but he couldn't form words.

"We're sorry." Marisa said for him.

Another pipe opened up and another eye came out, only this time it kept coming. It floated up a bit then was followed by one of the familiar hoof-like feet of the Gorgons. As it hit the floor more and more followed like yarn falling in a pile. Another eye, a mouth, a body, and finally the last leg came out forming a complete Gorgon. Without a word it stared at them and reached back into the pipe and pulled out a small ring of cloth and pulled it up its hind leg. Then it pulled out a body covering and threw it over its back. Only then did it look like a normal Gorgon to Joel and Marisa.

"Um." Said Joel, holding down the button. "We're sorry, we didn't mean to, um, disturb you."

"It's Okay. Shift starting now anyway." The translator said in halting tones.

The Gorgon looked at the other eye and walked away. The other eye snaked back into its pipe and the little hatch closed behind it, as did the hatch on the pipe that just ejected an entire Gorgon.

Joel let go of the button and took a few deep breaths, trying to calm himself. He leaned over to Marisa, who was busy doing the same, and said, "I think we just found their sleeping quarters."

"That was amazing." She replied, looking up and down the pipes. "They can uncurl."

"Yeah, it was, now let's get the hell out of here."

They headed back into the maze of corridors when another Gorgon appeared and walked towards them. For once Joel recognized it.

"Kevin?" he said. He could see a proper translator on his back.

"You really shouldn't be up here." Kevin replied.

"We're kinda lost."

"I figured. There's not much up here. Our rooms, nutrient areas, some recreation areas but I'm afraid we never thought you'd come here so your remotes were not programmed to work on these levels. I'll adjust them a little later for you."

"Oh, no, that's okay. We didn't mean to invade your privacy."

"Not at all. Here, I'll at least do yours, I know you are a curious people." He reached out and took Joel's remote and held down some buttons while pressing others then held it up towards a wall. A door opened and inside was just a small dark room that appeared to be empty. He pressed the closed button and handed it back to Joel. "Shhh." He said, "Our little secret. But you should let me show you the way out."

Joel nodded. "Thanks, because we really can't figure out where we are."

Joel and Marisa followed Kevin down the hallway.

"Kevin," Joel said, "I didn't know you could unravel."

One of Kevin's eyes turned around towards Joel. "Of course, how do you think we fit into our rooms?"

***

Matt poked his head into the window room and saw a woman sitting with a Gorgon.

"Oh, excuse me," he said. "I didn't mean to interrupt."

"Not at all, come on in." said Dr. Willhouse. "We were just shooting the breeze."

The Gorgon's eyes moved back and forth for a moment. "Actually, we were comparing our childhoods."

Matt walked in, followed by Melody. "I'm Matt, and this is my fiancé, Melody" he said, mainly because he didn't recognize either the Gorgon or the woman."

"Kay Willhouse"

"Ron."

Melody just looked around, wide eyed. Standing in front of so many stars with an alien and her future husband and another woman was just about overloading her senses. All she could manage was a nod.

"This is so unreal." She muttered.

"Isn't it?" said Dr. Willhouse. "You're the farmer, right? Ron here grew up on a farm."

"Really?" said Matt, taking a seat and motioning for Melody to sit. "I've seen your food, how, exactly, is that stuff harvested?"

"Oh, I didn't grow food, well, not for Gorgons. We had a small place for growing herbs for the dingles. Most houses have dingles, which I'm told is like a dog or, um…"

"Cat." Dr. Willhouse finished.

Matt smiled broadly, almost choking back a laugh. "These dingles," he started, then made a noise that sounded like air escaping from a balloon. Once he gathered himself he went on, oblivious of the stares he was getting, "Did they eat berries?" He could hold it no more and his shoulders moved up and down with a bout of laughter. Melody sat mortified, at first she didn't follow and then couldn't believe Matt would make a joke at the Gorgon's expense. Dr. Willhouse smiled and covered her mouth.

Ron looked back and forth at the humans. "Something is very funny but I cannot tell what. Does something funny happen when a dog eats a berry?"

"It would take a long time to explain. At least politely." Dr. Willhouse offered. "Suffice it to say Matt was being vulgar and, well, it was funny." Then quickly added, "In context."

They all fell silent and stared at the blue dot in the distance.

"You know," said Ron, "I've seen some movies and read up on your methods. I do not think we could teach you anything about farming. You seem to excel at it."

Matt nodded. "Thank you very much. But I have to say I'm surprised, coming from a race that figured out how to cross the universe."

"The galaxy." Ron corrected. "And even then only a small, small part of it."

After a few moments Ron stood up. "I need to go read up on a few things before this party. It's been a pleasure talking with you, Kay, and I really can't wait to see this icebreaker."

After the Gorgon walked out Matt turned to Dr. Willhouse and asked, "He does know there really won't be any ice there, doesn't he? I've heard other Gorgons talking."

"Oh. I don't know. He was entirely fascinating to talk with. I think they are just as amazed as we are about meeting another alien race. They just seem to hide it better."

Matt nodded. "The more I get to know them, the more they seem just like us."

"More than you'd think." Said Dr. Willhouse quietly. "Ron was telling me they have a training, much like our school, and when the time came he applied for crew aboard an exploration ship."

"He enlisted."

"Yes, kind of. Only he washed out twice and made it the third time. Just before this mission he was working for a mining crew, extracting ores from some moon when he overloaded a charge and blew apart an automated mining facility."

Matt chuckled. "I'll bet that's hard to live down."

"Must not have been too hard, he said he was pulled aside and offered this mission on a hush-hush basis. He's one of the crew that's been sneaking down to Earth to steal supplies."

Melody nodded, "Well, they did a good job there. No one saw any UFOs until they started picking up the models."

"According to Ron, raiding a warehouse is much easier than tracking down someone and picking them up. But he wasn't in on those missions. It's all rather fascinating, actually."

Matt leaned way back, stretched, and put his arm around Melody. "Yep, but we're the better farmers." He flashed a wide grin.

They all sat silent for a few moments then Dr. Willhouse, feeling like she was turning into a third wheel, excused herself.

Matt kissed Melody on the cheek then rested his head on hers. He didn't care where he was or what he was doing, he was just glad he was doing it with her.

Melody's thoughts, however, were being twisted by the idea that the man holding her right now was also responsible for eight other women being here, including her sister, and that he may have to one day sleep with them all.

29

"I cannot find a dress anywhere." Cindi plopped down in a recliner and let out a sigh. "Looks like it's going to be jeans and a t-shirt."

Karen and Becky exchanged glances. "What on earth do you need a dress for?"

Cindi rolled her eyes. "I want to look my best."

"Hoping to meet Mr. Right? Or did you just want to impress the aliens?"

"Looking your best isn't about impressing other people. It's about feeling confidence in yourself so you can put yourself out there and it's the confidence and poise that attract other people. It doesn't matter if they're men, women, or crunchy aliens. So the dress was for me, not for the benefit of others."

"I see." Said Karen, sarcastically. "It's just to get to know everybody. We may be spending a lot of time together."

Before Cindi could answer, Parminder wandered up and sat on the couch between Becky and Karen. "I hate this place, there is no sun light and everything is black, black, black."

Karen reached over and squeezed her shoulder. "Hang in there, Par, maybe this little party will cheer you up a little."

"I do not want to go. I do not want to meet anyone."

Even Cindi felt uncomfortable. Annie, who was rocking her baby in the next recliner over looked at Parminder. "If I have to go, you have to go. I'll need someone to sit in a corner with."

"Look," Karen said, trying to be diplomatic, "None of us asked to be here but here we are. Life is just a series of events, most of which we can't control. All we can control is how we react to it. Now here we are, floating in space on a bona-fide alien space ship with a bunch of other people who never asked to be here either and you may be bored, and sad, and upset, but keep in mind that we are unique, we are special. There are seven billion people on Earth, and only 33 are here, talking with aliens like some kind of movie. 33, out of seven billion. That makes us damn special. And forget dresses, and to hell with depression, I am damn glad I'm here. And I, for one, am going to thank Joel for bringing me here. If he hadn't picked up that damn calendar I'd still be rotting away in the hospital wishing I was dead."

Becky opened her mouth but Cindi beat her to it. "Well, good for you. And you may be right, we are special, and if we ever get back to Earth we'll all be famous. But right now, if things go as 'planned'" she made air quotes over the word 'planned', "we're going to be on our way to another planet, where all we'll be is baby incubator slaves for the Gorgon race. And we may be the Calendar Ten back on Earth, but what good is that if we're never going to see the place again?" None of which was what Becky was going to say at all.

Karen waved her hand. "Whatever. Did you ever talk with Terry or one of the other Gorgons? Halfway is green and beautiful, and they'll build us whatever kind of house we want, with whatever we want in it. It's not like we'll be living in tents in the desert. Why not have someone waiting on us hand and foot? We're saving their entire race for crying out loud, they're willing to do anything for us."

"Anything except let us go." Parminder put in. "I mean, really, how hard can it be to put me back and pick up someone else? Or pick up my husband and let it be our children that live in luxury? It cannot be hard at all."

Becky leaned back, this was a debate she didn't want to participate in but she still felt slightly guilty that she wasn't sticking up for her friend. She forced herself to say, "Well, I'm glad I'm here. I have nothing to lose."

Cindi flicked her hand. "Well, good for you."

"That was uncalled for." Karen snapped.

"Some of us did have things to lose." Cindi stood up stormed off. "Fuck you and your fucking attitude." She yelled as she disappeared behind some pallets of boxes.

"My attitude? Where does she get off? She's the one with the fucking attitude." Karen folded her arms and grunted. Deep breaths, let it go. She could almost hear her therapist's voice.

The angry silence was broken by a baby starting to cry.

Karen's tone changed completely. "Oh, god, I'm so sorry, I didn't mean…"

"It's okay," Annie assured her, "It was feeding time anyway. You can see why I think this party is going to be one big ball of fun." She got up and wandered off to someplace more private.

Three women sat on the couch and stared at the kitchen area.

"Oh, crap." Karen said suddenly, causing Parminder and Becky to look at her with questioning eyebrows. Karen looked back. "We were supposed to make a dish."

***

In a completely different kitchen area in a completely different hold five women stared at what was spread over the counter.

"Green Jell-O, whipped cream, and fruit cocktail. Surely we can do better than this." Betty idly poked a tub of whipped cream.

"We called that Ambrosia, but it needs marshmallows." Said Marie, who was secretly craving some.

"We used to call it half-an-hour-till-the-potluck-and-haven't-made-anything-yet." Donna, who had four kids had made this herself many times. Some of women nodded at her opinion of the food before them.

Isabel, a dark-skinned Mexican nurse who was still wearing the scrubs she was abducted in, decided to take charge. "Give me a half hour and I will whip up everything for some lovely fajitas. We will lay everything out, it will look and smell delicious."

The others nodded, that sounded perfectly alright. Tracy, who was content with just going along with everyone else was trying to picture what the models would come up with. She was nudged by Isabel.

"Down that way there were dry goods, I'm sure I saw shells and wraps. I would make sure we at least have twenty or so." It took a moment for Tracy to get back into the conversation, which wasn't lost on Isabel. "Are you doing okay? You seem a bit out of it."

Tracy forced a smile. "Yeah. Just wondering why we're here, you know? Wondering what my family is thinking. You know, nothing big."

Isabel bumped shoulders with her and smiled back, "Yeah, nothing big." They both forced a giggle.

Watching from across the counter Marie added, "Just saving the Gorgons and making national headlines and stuff. Nothing big at all."

"Do you really think we made national headlines?"

"Are you kidding? The first two groups were all over the news, they even pre-empted prime time. The president was supposed to say something tonight, I'm sure a third round of abductions really pushed the story over the edge."

"Actually," Donna said, "The last news I remember seeing was about people all over that were blaming disappearances going back years on the aliens. It may take a while for people to sort out that we really were taken."

With Cindi's words still ringing in her ears, Tracy looked at Donna, the largest of Matt's group, then at the rest and finally over her shoulder at Rachel, who was sitting on a small couch, staring off into the distance with a blank look on her face. She was becoming overwhelmed with things and the others were giving her some space. Why were they chosen and why would the news give them equal coverage when they could show ten bikini-clad models or ten brilliant, accomplished women?

"In any case, ladies, chop, chop." Isabel clapped her hands. "I, for one, want to make sure everyone knows that group three, that's us," she pointed around the counter, "brings the best dish. Now here's what we need…"

**

"I've talked with Larry," Gary announced, "And when things start dying down tonight they will show some videos from Gorgon, and I just can't wait to see them. I can't even fathom what it's going to look like."

"Well," said Dr. Willhouse, "We at least know they have farms. And they build at right angles, and a few other things. I can't wait, either."

They all sat in their little circular common area in various chairs and couches and nodded in agreement. This was most exciting.

"I wonder if in a social setting they'll be open to talk." Said Dr. Collum.

"I think they are open to talk, it just seems like no one knows anything." Added Nola. "Every time I ask how something works they just tell me about what buttons they press and what happens as a result. No one seems to know how things actually function." A general murmur indicated that this was indeed what everyone was experiencing.

Amber just sat there, a little bewildered, she still wasn't sure what her part in all this was. Gary just wished he could get her alone for just five minutes but it seemed like every time he tried something else came up.

"Hopefully we'll learn something tonight." Gary said, then thought for a moment and added, "Did we make anything? For the pot luck, that is."

No one said anything, it was the last thing on their minds. Nola was the first to offer a suggestion. "Well, I would could make some whipped fluff, with some fruit in it. We would just need some Jell-O and whipped cream."

"Oh, god, no." one of the others said.

"Okay," said Chase, "I'm just throwing this out there. I saw a big pile of Tuna Helper boxes and I'm sure there's tuna somewhere, we'll just make a bunch of that and no one will be the wiser."

"Well, that is basically a casserole, I have no problems with that."

Gary spotted another moment. "Amber, why don't you and I go find some tuna fish. They have tons of canned goods."

Amber looked around at the women who were just standing up, some brushing the wrinkles out of their clothes, some gathering up tea cups and spoons, and then back at Gary who was still waiting for a reply and something clicked. For the moment she wasn't sure if she was flattered or creeped out by the thoughts going through her head.

***

"So you see," Joel was saying, "I cut them in half before I fry them. Keep draining the grease, and you have perfect bread sized bacon."

Marissa nodded. "But with lettuce and tomato we'll need toast. And you just can't pre-make toast. It gets all stale."

"I think it's perfect all by itself with ketchup and mayo, or on top of a runny egg." He picked up a perfectly crisp piece of bacon and popped it in his mouth. "Or just plain."

The men's hold was empty except for Joel and Marissa playfully frying bacon at each other. There were already several plates heaped with various brands and crispness scattered around the stove area. They had convinced themselves that it wouldn't go to waste as they would present it at the pot luck, and they had equally convinced themselves that none would be left.

Marissa looked at an empty wrapper and pondered the brand. "I don't think we have this around, er, that is, back in Wakely. It's pretty good." She thought about her small town and the grubby little supermarket and how she would never walk into it again. Sometimes the thought that she would visit after a few years, or show her kids, would cross her mind but she would abruptly stop when she remembered that there was no way to go back.

Somehow, Joel saw all of that in her eyes.

Not knowing what to say Joel just pressed on. "We should make a heaping plate of sliced tomatoes and a bowl of lettuce. Just in case."

"Yeah."

"You okay?"

"Yeah, it's just, well, I don't normally go to parties."

"Why not? I would have thought you go all the time."

"Not a lot of parties in a small town. Maybe a super bowl party or two, Christmas, Fourth of July. But never just a party where people have fun for no reason."

"This isn't just any party. I keep thinking about it. We're in space, with aliens, on a spaceship. If these ceilings weren't so low I'd love to see fireworks and a big disco ball, and actually see the Gorgons cutting loose. It's the dawn of a new age..."

"Hey, don't think about it too much. For all we know everyone will just stand around staring at each other."

Joel smiled, "I can't see you just standing around. I'll bet you're the life of the party."

"Until some saucy little Miss June comes up, I'm sure."

"Aww, give me a break. I should have picked ten of you." It took Joel a few moments to realize what he had just said. He looked at her smiling and blushing, idly slicing a tomato, and thought that yes, he really meant it.

***

Sixteen Gorgons sat in a pool of nutrients and murmured to each other in voices that no human could hear.

"So, they each bring food, which they chew up in their mouths, and this is supposed to start conversations."

"Why don't they just introduce themselves? What's so hard with just saying, 'Hello, I'm Craig from Verbrom and I work with coolants.'?"

"Quite frankly, I don't know. It's just how they socialize." Kevin again felt like he wasn't doing his job but there was still so much about humans that didn't make sense. "Look at it this way, we are taking in nutrients and discussing things, that's basically what they'll be doing. At first the theory was that as they grind up different foods in their mouths it made their breath smell differently, so people from different areas would feel more at home if visitors had familiar smelling breath but now we just think they need something to keep them occupied while they think of something to say."

"It just seems like a waste of resources to me. Unless they don't eat prior so they actually need the food."

"Oh, they digest just about everything they eat, no matter when they eat it or why."

A Gorgon at the far end piped up, "Well, at this rate we'll need to fill another hold with food. Just to be sure. What do you think, Bob?"

Bob didn't hear his name at first as he was staring at Tom sitting across from him. He was only slightly embarrassed when nudged back into the conversation.

"Just get a list." He said, not fully aware of what was said. Some Gorgons tried to stifle a chuckle. He perked up just a little. "In any case, it's a night off, we socialize, maybe learn a little, then it's back to the last few trips down to the planet and then we prepare for space. I'm sure we're all looking forward to getting back home."

A general murmur of agreement filled the room. They would be welcomed back as heroes, the Gorgons who took the first steps in saving their race.

Only one Gorgon sat silent, and wondered if would ever see his home world again.

30

"I am filled with great pride looking out at all of you today. I am looking forward to getting to know you all, and having you all getting to know us." Bob's four eyes scanned the audience, he could tell the other Gorgons were waiting politely but had no idea how to read the humans. "Some of us have gathered some home movies and it's been decided we should all introduce ourselves, but I've been informed that it may take quite a while and humans prefer their food warm. So please, mix it up, break some ice, get to know a few others, and, by all means, have a pleasant time."

The short platform that Bob had been standing on lowered itself into the floor as thirty three humans and nearly two hundred Gorgons looked around, wondering what to do next.

Gary started clapping and the rest of the humans joined in. Startled, the Gorgons all suddenly looked at Kevin, who was supposed to know what the humans were doing and at first he froze with all the eyes he was suddenly faced with, then he collected himself and started clapping, too, which didn't make much noise given the construction of his hands. The other Gorgons started to catch on and soon the whole room was filled with muffled applause.

Then, like a bunch of 8th graders at their first dance, nothing happened.

Joel, Gary, and Matt exchanged glances.

Matt smacked his hands together and said, "Well…" causing the other two to jump. "I'm not proud, let's eat." He led Melody up to the table where all the food had been laid out and they started filling their plates. Joel followed with Marisa in tow and soon most of the humans had bacon and fajitas and some even had bacon fajitas, with tuna casserole on the side.

The Gorgons watched the strange ritual unfold before them and it looked vaguely familiar. They often soak in groups why shouldn't humans eat in groups?

It was Dr. Cheng and Dr. Willhouse who first saddled up to two Gorgons sitting at a round table near the front.

"I don't believe we've met." Said Dr. Cheng. They exchanged hellos and the Gorgons introduced themselves as Richard and Jeff and after that the table fell silent again.

"Well," said Dr. Willhouse, "now we've broken the ice, so to speak. What do you two gentlemen do aboard this ship?"

"Ah…" Said Richard. "Breaking the ice does mean introductions. I was just telling Jeff that."

Jeff's eyes were scanning the women up and down. "If you don't mind, how do keep your balance so well?"

"Good question. We have these organs in our ears that detect motion, and together with visual cues they cause minute muscle movements that keep us balanced. It works like this…"

Other Gorgons started to gather around to listen to the explanation which totally fascinated them. Humans actually have tubes of fluid in their heads. This led to other questions which the two doctors gladly answered. Even some of the other women joined in with some questions which confused the Gorgons even more.

"You mean you have these things in your body and you don't know how they work?" asked one.

"Well, I'm sure there are many things in my body that I don't know exactly how it works. I mean, I know generally how things work but not every single little thing. Do you know how every little part of your body works?"

"I see your point." Said Richard. "But this balancing organ sound like a major part, as does the hearing and the whole skull thing in general. It seems like everything is in that thing."

Around the room similar groups had formed. Matt and Melody were cheerfully describing various television shows and one group was discussing the basic office setup and meeting protocols, and yet another were having a serious discussion on Greek mythology.

Parminder, however, found a quiet corner and sat with Annie who was quietly rocking Josie. Many Gorgons were dying to ask about the baby but instinctively knew that she didn't want to take part in any major discussion. A subgroup formed instead and Betty and Isabel, from Matt's group, found themselves explaining babies and having Gorgon babies explained to them.

However, Terry felt the need to check on her and quietly walked up. "You two don't seem to be eating like the others."

"I am not especially hungry." Parminder said.

Their earlier meeting ran through Terry's mind. "I just wanted to say I would have done things differently had I been the one making the decisions."

"It's okay." Was all she could think to say.

Josie chose that moment to start fussing and Annie bounced her a little on her knee and couldn't help noticing Terry staring at the baby. She considered very carefully her next words, she wasn't sure what Terry would think. "Would you like to hold her?"

The translator on Terry's back actually purred. At first Annie thought it was some kind of static but she wasn't so sure it was just picking up on a noise Terry was making. "Well, I…um…"

Very nervously Annie stood up and became aware of gradual quieting of the general hub-bub around the room. She tried not to look at all the eyes turning towards them.

"Okay," she said with a quiver in her voice. "She's just a baby, you can't break her. Just hold her body like this." She carefully showed Terry how she was holding her.

Parminder put her hands up to her mouth, being nervous for all them.

Terry reached out with his bendy arms then pulled them back, reached out again in another way and pulled back again. He spread his front legs out to steady himself and tried again.

"Don't worry, I trust you."

With that Terry very carefully lifted Josie out of Annie's arms. He gently brought her to his body and lowered his mouth stalk underneath, like a third arm. His boneless arms seemed to form a soft cradle and Josie almost smiled and kicked a bit. Four eyes nearly curled up on top of her as he tried to fathom the young human in his arms.

The whole room was nearly silent and those furthest back were crowding up to see what all the fuss was about. No one dared come any nearer to the scene, though, as if they knew it was something they were just meant to witness and not take part in. A small, very quiet round of applause went up and Annie blushed. Terry, realizing he was the center of attention, turned towards the crowd.

"I'm holding a baby." Was all he could think to say.

Gary took a step forward and raised his glass. "I'd like to propose a toast." He said loudly, then paused for a moment until he could see most of the humans finding glasses of their own. "To the first ever meeting of our two great races. As Bob said before, this is truly a momentous occasion. We are not alone." He raised his glass, "Cheers."

A tiny chorus of "here, here" and tinkling glasses drifted around the room as the aliens looked on in wonder.

"Weirdest thing I ever saw." Quietly came out of one the translators which prompted a round of giggles and then conversations started up again. Terry carefully handed Josie back to her mother.

He lowered his eyes and pressed his arms to his body in what almost looked like a bow. "It was indeed an honor. Thank you. On Gorgon only special friends and family would ever hold a child."

"Any time, Terry."

"Do you have family?" Parminder asked.

"Yes, I do."

"Why don't you have a seat and tell us about them?"

Around the room groups reformed and without anyone realizing it, hours began to pass.

***

Dr. Collum and Dr. Plaitte retreated to one of the walls that were placed around the outside of the room. It was just the right height to lean on and watch the party evolve before them.

"Best party I've been to in ages." Dr. Collum said. "Can you imagine if there was actually alcohol here?"

Dr. Plaitte chuckled. "There is, somewhere. And this is the party of the year." Then, after thinking a moment, "Party of the millennium, really."

"Yeah. I just talked with, um, didn't catch the name actually, but a Gorgon who works with food, or whatever it is they soak in. It was kind of odd."

"In what way?"

"Well, for starters, he was telling a story about how he accidently mixed some chemicals in a food supply for some exploratory mission. They barely made it back alive when he discovered a back up supply that he neglected to record in his inventory. They were sitting on enough food and didn't even know it."

"Just sounds like a funny mix up."

"Yeah, but why would he be chosen for this mission? I would have knocked him back to janitor. And I keep asking but no one seems to know how the gravity works."

Before Dr. Plaitte could reply another woman walked behind the wall. "Mind if I join you?"

"Oh, not at all."

"Marie," she said, holding out her hand. "From the brawn group, at least that's what I heard someone calling us." Some contempt was seeping out with her voice.

"You must have been talking to some beauties. They seem to think they're special."

"Yeah." Marie smiled a little bit. "I was just over there, where what's her name is telling Gorgons not just why women wear makeup but how to put it on. I'm sure they can use the information."

"Heh, and here I was worried about the gravity."

"Is there something wrong with the gravity?"

"No, I just want to know how it works."

The three women stared out for a few more moments. Marie sighed and said, "Boy, I could sure use a cigarette. I only have one left and I'm saving it."

"I quit about three years ago and I still crave them." Dr. Collum rested her head on her hands, she was starting to feel a little tired.

"I've searched every hold." Marie went on, "Nada. Not so much as a match. Good thing I had my lighter on me as well."

Dr. Plaitte smiled. "Just don't smoke in front of one of these aliens, it may freak them out. They are kind of plant based, I think."

After a few more moments Marie said, "It's been nice meeting you. I think I'm going to get some more punch, or whatever it is."

The two doctors leaned on the wall on some more and tried to pick up snippets of conversations that were going on around them. Suddenly, Dr. Plaitte stood up straight and slapped the top of the wall, startling Dr. Collum.

"Did she say she smoked cigarettes? I mean, did she say she did after she got here? Or just that she had one left?"

Shaking her head Dr. Collum replied, "I'm not sure, she kind of implied that she did."

She looked at Dr. Plaitte, still not sure what seemed so excited about. They just stared at each other a bit.

"Come on, we've got to find her."

Grabbing Dr. Collum by the arm, Dr. Plaitte rushed out into the room. Marie wasn't hard to find and Dr. Plaitte grabbed her arm as well and said, "Can we talk to you in the hall? It's urgent." Without waiting for an answer led her to the doorway.

Once outside she looked around anxiously and then asked, "Do you have your lighter on you?" Marie nodded. "Great, come with me."

"Am I in some kind of trouble? I didn't mean to..."

"No." was all Dr. Plaitte said. She led them down the hall into the next storage room all the while looking around. Once in the middle of the room, surrounded by boxes and out of sight, acting like a giddy school girl she said, "Let me see it, let me see it."

Marie pulled the lighter out of her pocket and handed it over to Dr. Plaitte, who immediately lit it. All three women stared at the flame. "Don't you see?" She said, excitedly.

Dr. Collum raised an eyebrow. "It's a lighter."

"No, look!" Dr. Plaitte looked around and then quickly tore a corner off the nearest box. She lit the cardboard and dropped it on the floor, then crouched over it, as if she's never seen a fire before. "Don't you see? It's burning normally." She stood up and stepped the cardboard out.

The other two women continued to stare blankly at her. Finally she realized that she wasn't getting through. "It's fire! Don't you see? The Gorgons told us there was no oxygen in this atmosphere. If there was no oxygen then a fire couldn't burn. They said they changed our bodies to not need oxygen, that there was no oxygen in this air. They said we'd suffocate if we went back."

Dr. Collum made a long "Oooohhhh" sound. "That was the one thing we couldn't figure out how they did it, and it's probably because they didn't do it."

Now Dr. Plaitte was smiling and nodding frantically. Suddenly she paused and pointed right at Marie's face. "Don't breathe a word of this to anyone. We don't know how the Gorgons might react to being caught in a lie. Right now, I don't think there's anything stopping us from going home."

***

Gary didn't notice three women returning to the room as he finally made his way towards Amber. As casually as he could he stood next to her and asked her how she was doing.

"Oh, fine." She said. "Actually, it's quite fascinating. They have a sort of democracy but it's layered. Gorgons are voted in to lower levels and then to higher levels of government. They all have to literally start at the bottom and prove themselves to move on."

"That's kind of neat." Gary nodded a few times not sure what else to say.

"Gary," said Amber, looking down. "Do you mind if I ask you something?

"Sure, anything."

"Why did you bring me aboard?"

This caught Gary a little by surprise. "Well, like I said, I was hoping to find a way off this ship and I thought one person, a lobbyist, who uses persuasion for a living, might come in handy. That is, I tried to pick a variety of women, to, uh, well, just in case."

"But how do you even know who I am?"

"I saw you on CNN a few times. And there was a dinner in Delaware that my company sponsored, you gave a speech on the importance of corporate sponsorship."

Still staring at the floor Amber considered this. "I'm not a lobbyist."

"I'm sorry?" Gary's eyebrows went high on his forehead.

"I'm not a lobbyist. I'm a grant writer. CNN labeled me a lobbyist because that's what they wanted on the panel. It was just a part I played, really."

"But I thought you were. I don't know what to say."

"If you had researched me, even a little, I think that would have been apparent. And there are many other women out there who can be much more persuasive than a lobbyist. What about a lawyer or saleswoman?"

"I didn't have much time to think things through." Gary lied. "I was just going off the cuff."

Maybe she had it wrong, thought Amber.

"Besides," added Gary, trying to sound just a little macho, "I thought you were someone I'd really like to meet."

There it was. Maybe she had it right after all. "So you didn't pick me because you thought you needed me." Her voice got a little louder and she finally looked him in the eye.

Before he could answer loud angry voices from across the room grabbed their attention.

Cindi and Alicia sat on some stools near a wall looking very much like the models they were supposed to be. Alicia liked the audience that formed around which included several Gorgons leaning on the wall with Captain White and Tatyana from Gary's group and Rachel and Tracy from Matt's.

"So you see," she was saying, "All a woman has to do is wiggle her legs," she wiggled her legs, "and then a man turns to putty in her hands."

"Oh yes," one Gorgon said. "We are quite the admirers of legs ourselves." A general chuckle went around the group.

"And these, too." Both Alicia and Cindi smiled and pressed their arms together and wiggled their shoulders to highlight their cleavage. More chuckles.

"We don't have those." Another Gorgon said.

"Not all women have them, either." Alicia smiled and flipped her hair back.

"Then it's back to the legs."

"Oh, now," piped up Captain White, "There's also personality and intelligence." She flashed her smile around to keep the mood light.

Cindi rolled her eyes. "Yeah, for when a woman doesn't have these." She kicked one of her legs out and wiggled her foot.

"Maybe for a shallow guy." Said Tracy. The two women locked eyes.

"For any guy. He's going to look at some legs before he looks for personality."

"But then all he'll find is an empty shell."

"At least I'm never lonely late at night."

"At least a guy stays with me for more than three minutes."

"At least I can walk by a McDonalds without losing my breath."

"At least I can make change without counting on my fingers."

The insults got louder and louder and they were attracting the attention of others around the room. The Gorgons, who were enjoying the banter at first started to feel uneasy and backed off a few steps.

Captain White stepped between them. In her firm authoritative voice she said, "Alright, back off, both of you."

Tracy took a step forward and Cindi stood up.

"At least I'm not a thirty year old virgin." Sniped Cindi, ignoring Captain White.

Joel and Marissa came up at that point and Joel grinned a fake grin. "Ladies, ladies, please, what's going on here?"

"I'm just about to hand little Miss January her teeth."

"I was Miss April!"

"Like I care!"

They each took another step but Karen and Becky, who had just arrived stepped in front of Cindi, and Joel and Marissa took a position in front of Tracy. Captain White stood in between.

"It's just like a brawn to be jealous."

Karen turned and pointed at Cindi's face, "Look," she said sternly, "you need to lay off the brawn shit. There are no names, we're just groups one, two, and three."

"Damn right we're number one."

Tracy lunged but between Joel, Marissa and Captain White they held her back.

"Just stop!" Captain White yelled.

"Back off, Poindexter." Tracy yelled back.

"Poindexter?"

Matt and Gary pushed their way in.

Cindi was still yelling. "You're just jealous because Joel is the only man here with taste."

Joel turned around, still holding one of Tracy's arms. "Taste? You guys won't even talk to me."

"Just because we hate you doesn't mean you don't have taste."

Karen slapped her forehead. "That's the stupidest thing I've ever heard."

"Whose side are you on anyway?"

"I just don't want a fight breaking out."

Alicia put her hand on Cindi's shoulder, "Come on, we're too classy for this bullshit. Just turn your back."

Cindi shook off the arms that were around and stood up straight. She turned around and was surprised to see almost all her group standing behind her. She glanced at the door just in time to see Parminder and Annie walking out with the baby. "You're right." She said. "Let's go leave these brawns to the banquet."

With that Tracy lunged again and Captain White was half inclined to let her go but together with Joel and Marissa held her back. Looking behind her she could see some others from Matt's group were visibly angry and pushing forward.

"ALLRIGHT, THAT'S ENOUGH."

The whole room froze with the sheer power and anger from Matt's voice.

He pointed his fingers in two directions and yelled again, "Everyone go back to their holds, you first." He pointed at Joel's group. He had experience breaking up fights and knew better than to have them all funnel through the door at once. "Joel, make sure they all go back. Gary, take your group back."

Gary nodded and awkwardly waved a follow-me wave and led his group towards the door.

At this point most of the Gorgons had backed off to a safe distance leaving Bob and Kevin standing next to Matt. Bob's eyes were bobbing and weaving frantically.

"Melody, would you mind?" She just nodded and led the last of the women out.

In a moment he was the only human left in the room.

"What in the name of Gorgon just happened?" Even the translator seemed to be scared.

"Just a little fight. Welcome to the human race." Frustrated, Matt walked over to the buffet table, picked up a plate of bacon, and walked out of the room.

Nearly two hundred Gorgons stood there in silence until a sudden round of muffled applause went up.

Kevin waved his hands in the air. "No! Not now." He said, and then walked out himself.

Bob looked around the room and had no idea what to say. After a long pause he stood tall and looked at all his shipmates staring at him.

"Well, I guess the ice has been broken."

31

Joel followed the women into their hold and stood there and watched as they plopped down in various chairs. He felt he ought to say something but was entirely uncertain as to what.

"Look, while it's true you were the first aboard and you are, well, models..."

Before he could finish Karen came up and pushed him out of the door and closed it, wishing it would slam.

As he stared at the smooth wall he heard a giggle from down the hall. Turning around he saw Marissa smiling at him.

"Well, it looks like the man with taste got kicked out again."

Joel smiled back. "Just because I have taste doesn't mean they can't hate me."

"Is that your remote in your pocket, or are you just happy to see me?"

Trying to hold back a giggle himself, Joel pulled the remote out of his pocket.

Marissa smiled more broadly. "I happen to know most of the Gorgons have the night off, would you like to take a walk? I was thinking this time we'd go down, find the engine room or something."

Glancing back over his shoulder he mused, "Well, the sister wives don't seem to mind…"

She punched him in the shoulder. "Not even funny. Let's go."

A few moments later they were walking down a spiraling hallway which they could only assume was the way down. Every once in a while Joel would hit the door open button to see if anything was nearby but the only rooms they passed so far were blank and small and didn't seem to serve any purpose.

"You know," said Marissa, "There should at least be control rooms, or mechanical rooms, or something. How to do they run things? How do they fix things?"

"They are aliens, everything they do can be alien to us, even how they build ships."

"You've been hanging out with the brains too much."

"Actually, I came up with that one all on my own." He pressed the button again.

This time they immediately saw something different.

"Finally, some action."

The room was about twenty feet long with square windows along one wall. Under the windows were slanted panels with displays and buttons, all smooth and subdued. Some displays scrolled the strange alien language and some seem to flash just one character at a time. It all looked very complicated.

Joel put his hand on Marissa's shoulder. "Don't touch anything." He said, very, very seriously. She nodded in agreement.

Even more amazing than the control panels was what they saw through the windows. It was a large bay with twenty flying saucers lined up two by two, each on three skinny legs. Cables and pipes were hooked up to a few and there were even some things that looked like carts here and there. All the walls and ceilings were smooth and it was hard to see where they would exit.

"Now that's what I'd like to see." Marissa said in awe. "Can you see a way down?"

Joel tried to make a mental map of the hallway, the walls, the bay, and couldn't connect one to the other. On a whim he pointed his remote to the far side of the control room and hit the open door button.

A door opened. They hurriedly looked inside but it was just another tiny room, barely big enough for a closet.

Being very careful not to touch anything on the panels Joel put his hand down so he could lean towards the windows for a downward view. Directly below this room was what looked like a counter or wall that curved out in a half circle from the wall. Looking around he couldn't see a half circle anywhere else in the bay.

Marissa slapping his arm startled him out of his train of thought.

"It's an elevator!" She grabbed his arm and practically pulled him into the little room.

He hit the door close button and waited. Nothing happened. He hit the door open button and they were still at the control room.

"It's a nice thought," he said, "but there are no up or down buttons on the remote. And no buttons I can see in the elevator."

"It must be one of these…" Marissa started to examine the panel closest to the elevator.

"Really, I don't think we should mess with that. What if we launch an invasion or something?"

"Look, this is it, I'll bet you." At the furthest right, almost by itself, was a square light on top of a long line. She touched the box, and an outline formed around it.

"Oh, jeeze…" Joel looked around nervously.

She slid the box down the line. In unison, they looked up to see the door close. After a few seconds Joel pointed his remote at it and hit the door open button. Nothing happened. At that same moment the box slid back up the line and once at the top the door opened again.

"HA!" Marissa yelled.

Okay," said Joel, "I am really impressed with you right now. You have single handedly figured out an alien elevator." He pointed the remote at the door they came in and closed it.

They locked eyes for a moment.

"You know, I meant what I said. I wish I had picked ten of you."

"That's very sweet." She leaned in. He leaned in. Then they finally kissed.

Marissa started grinning mid kiss and backed away. "I have a wicked idea."

She pushed him into the elevator, slid the box down the line, then jumped in after him.

A few moments later a different door opened and they found themselves looking into the largest room they'd seen yet. It actually felt refreshing after the low ceilings of all the holds and hallways.

As they walked out Joel looked at the half circle counter and could see a line of the carts along the back wall. "I think it's a tool check out or something. Like in a garage."

The saucers were about four times as large as the one Joel remembered hovering over his car, but still looked like something from a bad science fiction movie. For a brief moment he wondered about his car, and his classes, and his friends and wondered if they had any idea what happened to him, or if they missed him at all.

Marissa yanked him back into reality. "Come on." She was already in the middle of the bay.

"Just how big is this ship?" Joel mumbled as he walked out. He stopped at one the trays and was amazed at what he saw. "Look!" he said, holding up a flat screwdriver. There were wrenches and pliers that, while obviously made differently, were almost like the ones on Earth. Among them were other boxes and motors that he couldn't recognize at all, some with tiny lights and buttons on them.

"Come on." Marissa said, a bit more sternly. "I want to see the inside of one of these."

Again Joel's sense of caution kicked in, but as long as they didn't touch anything what's the worst that could happen?

Together they walked to nearly the far end of the hold. "None of them seem to be opened, and I'm not sure where the doors would be on them anyway."

They walked back and picked one that had twice the number of carts under it as well as cables and hoses plugged into it. Joel ran his hand over the cold hard surface and couldn't feel so much as a rivet.

"Try the remote."

Joel pointed the remote at the saucer and pressed the door open button. For a moment he didn't notice that it lit up yellow.

"That's odd." He said. "I've never seen a button light up before."

"There must be some way. I was hoping we could, you know, make out in the back seat."

Joel grinned. "Oh, you are wicked. Like the car in Titanic."

Marissa raised an eyebrow. "Please don't compare this ship to the Titanic."

"Well, it's gotta open now." He pointed the remote up again and hit the door open button again. This time it turned red. Joel looked at it. "I have a bad feeling about this."

"Alright." Marissa admitted that it didn't seem right to her either. Looking around one last time they walked back over to the counter.

"How about the elevator?"

"Oh," Marissa grinned. "It will be my third time in an elevator."

Joel smiled and pointed the remote at the wall and hit the door open button again.

Before he could ask her about the first two times a loud roar echoed around the bay and his ears instantly popped. Instinctively he dropped the remote and pressed his palms against his ears, he could see Marissa doing the same.

At the far end of the hold the wall was dropping down from the ceiling and beyond...stars.

A sudden gust of air lifted them both towards the center of the hold then dropped them again. Marissa slid against the far wall and Joel was knocked into one of the legs of a flying saucer. He could feel thumping in his skull and chest and didn't realize it was Gorgon alarms going off. He looked around frantically for the remote when a pain shot across his chest.

He realized he couldn't breathe. All the air was gone out of the hold. Lights started flashing in his eyes as tried to find where Marissa had landed.

Against the far wall she, too, was gasping for air. Joel's mind was reeling. He wanted to go to her but knew if the door wasn't closed they'd both die. The flashing in his eyes were almost blinding but he could see some of the saucers silently coming apart. It was like a dream. The bottom dropped out of one, one was cracking in half, one had dropped to the floor. All too silently.

The remote. He had to find it. He could see hands around him and bobbing eyes. He felt like he was flying.

Then, darkness.

***

"Matt," Melody said, after they had settled into their own hold, "I want to ask you something personal, and I want you to answer honestly."

This never goes well, thought Matt. "Anything, pumpkin." They faced each other on either side of a couch and Matt could see something was bothering her.

After composing her thoughts she figured she would just come out and ask. "Why did you pick those women?"

Matt knew this question was coming sooner or later, but this was much sooner than he had hoped. "Well," he said slowly, trying to find the right words. "I just wanted to pick women that were worse than you." Melody's jaw dropped and Matt instantly recognized that he had picked the wrong words. "Not worse than you, I meant not as attractive as you. I mean, I didn't want you to think I was taking advantage of the situation."

"So, you don't think any of those women are pretty?"

Matt sensed he was walking into a trap but continued anyway. "No."

"But they all look like me!"

"No, no they don't. I made sure they were at least heavier."

"Heavier!?"

"No, that's not what I meant."

"What exactly do you mean?"

"Look, like I said, I didn't want you to get jealous. If I had picked nine models like Joel did you would probably hate me."

"So, you don't think I'm as pretty as Joel's models?"

Matt shook his head in frustration. "This is something I will never win at. All I wanted was you. I was forced to pick nine others, that's all. Other than Kim and the baby I told them to pick totally at random."

"Just heavier?"

"Like I said, I didn't want you to think I was taking advantage of anything." He paused. "Do you hear a bass drum?"

"Never mind that. I just want to know what you were thinking."

"Okay, here's the thing, I love you. I will always love you. I think you are the most beautiful person the planet and now you are the most beautiful woman in space. That's all that matters to me. I wanted you here with me, and no one else."

"Matt, I love you, too." They slid up next to each other and started to kiss. They didn't even notice a Gorgon, Joe, come running through the door.

"Matt," Joe yelled, startling both humans to their feet. "There's been an accident, you'd better come with me."

***

Gary sat at the counter with several of his group sitting around him excitedly discussing the oxygen in the atmosphere.

"How did you find this out?"

Dr. Plaitte, who could barely maintain her composure told him. "One of the brawns had a lighter." Gary frowned at her. "Okay, one of group three had a lighter. She was a smoker and had a lighter on her."

Dr. Collum added, "We burned some cardboard, there's definitely oxygen here. Fire won't burn without it."

"Won't fire burn with other gasses? Like besides oxygen?"

"No."

There was a few moments while everyone pondered.

"Okay, let's think," said Gary. "Do we confront them with this or just move on and try to find a way back down to Earth?"

"I don't know. I don't know." Dr. Plaitte was still very excited.

"Why would they lie to us?"

"Well, that's obvious. They don't want us to leave. They didn't want to force us to stay so they made this up so that we'd give up wanting to go back."

They all paused for a moment. "Do you feel that?" said Gary. "It's like a deep bass subwoofer."

They all agreed that they felt it.

The door went up and Kevin ran in causing several of the women to jump.

"As I understand it," Kevin said excitedly, "one of you is a doctor. There's been an accident. I'm afraid Joel has been hurt."

Dr. Cheng jumped up, "Where did I see those first aid kits?"

***

Joe the Gorgon led Matt down some winding corridors to where a small crowd had gathered. Bob and Kevin were there as were many Matt didn't recognize. It was mostly silent except for Joel, who was curled up on the floor sobbing.

Matt knelt and put his hand on Joel's shoulder and looked around for any signs of injuries.

Quietly he leaned over and asked Joel what happened, but all Joel could say was, "She's gone, she's gone..."

Another hand came down on Matt's shoulder, it was Bob. His translator spoke quietly. "Joel was in the hanger with the freighters. We're not sure how, but the bay doors were opened."

Matt looked up. "Who was in there with him?"

"We're not sure."

"Marissa." Matt looked down, he knew they had been spending time together. "Joel," he said calmly and quietly, "Was Marissa in there with you?"

This brought a new round of sobbing but Joel was at least able to nod his head yes.

Gary and Dr. Cheng knelt behind Matt. Behind them several other women and Gorgons were coming in. Gary stood up and pulled Bob to one side and asked what happened.

"We're not sure how it happened," Bob explained again. "His remote shouldn't have been able to open the bay doors at all." He took a few more steps away. "Gary, I'm sorry. The bay had twenty freighters in it and they weren't prepped for space. When the bay doors opened some of the freighters depressurized explosively. That was when Carl and Evan, who were working on one, found Joel. Unfortunately they didn't see anyone else in the hanger." Bobs eyes hung a little bit lower. "There was a fuel spill, the fuel is very corrosive, it started melting into the walls and floor. Once the hanger was sealed the computer completed an emergency flush of the entire hanger. It had to be done to save the ship." After a long pause he added, "Everything was washed into space…everything"

"Oh, that poor girl." Melody had heard the whole story and was tearing up behind Gary.

"We don't know how it could have happened, even my remote shouldn't open the bay doors."

With his eyes hung low Kevin faced Bob. "I'm afraid this may have been my fault."

Everyone looked up at him.

"They were walking around before, so I reprogrammed their remote to a general crew level so they could see other parts of the ship. However, that shouldn't have been able to open the bay doors either."

Bob lifted his eyes and faced Kevin. "Find one of the programmers. I want an immediate review of all doors and permissions. Change the codes on all external doors so that no one can open them except bay commanders and then I want to see them all a little later."

"I'll do it myself." And with that Kevin turned and headed up the corridor.

Another Gorgon walked up. "I'm so sorry, Gary. We didn't see anyone else in the bay. She must have been behind something. You know we would have given our lives to save her had we known she was there."

Bob introduced Carl to Gary. For the first time Gary noticed half the Gorgon's cover was torn away, and the side of his body was discolored and appeared burned in places.

"Are you okay?" Gary asked.

"Oh, yes. Evan and I will be okay. We're just so terribly sorry." His eyes drooped almost past his body.

"It's okay, it's not your fault. You did what you could." Gary bent over a little bit to look in his eyes. "You saved Joel, we thank you for that. On our world you would be called a hero."

"I sure don't feel like a hero."

"Carl, take Evan and go to hospital before those get worse." Bob actually patted Carl on the back and sent him away.

Gary walked over and waved Dr. Cheng back and knelt down next to his friend. Matt was trying to calm him down but it didn't seem to be doing any good.

Together the two men helped Joel to his feet and escorted him through the sea of Gorgons and women who all came to see what was going on.

32

Bob paced back and forth across his quarters. Even though it was exactly the same as the other senior staff's quarters Kevin couldn't help but think that it was different somehow. It seemed more open and friendlier, but it had to be all in his brain coil, he thought.

In their own language with no translators, Bob asked Kevin what he had found.

"Well," started Kevin, hesitantly, "The permissions and hierarchy in the main systems is just a mess. The ones who set it up didn't take into account the different layers of management or duty rosters. I hate to say this…"

After a look from Bob he went on. "But I think our resident security expert and his assistant were totally incompetent. A third level student could have set things up better. Most of the remotes had outer door privileges but no one knew that. There were still three steps but Joel wouldn't have known that, it seems he was trying to open the elevator at the time but the remote had already locked onto the bay doors."

Bob lowered his eyes and stared at nothing in particular. "We lost twenty freighters, there are only four left. All three groups gave us lists and there are still nineteen empty holds. The window for the leap to Halfway is not a long one. Everything is falling apart."

Not entirely, Kevin thought to himself.

"Gather everyone in an empty hold, we shall mourn the loss of the human as if she were one of our own. Tell the humans it's mandatory, we don't have time to waste on bickering like they did at the ice breaker."

"Bob, I don't think that's a good idea. We should concentrate on our last supply runs."

Bob's eyes raised in surprise. "Nonsense. I have come to think of Matt, Gary, and Joel as my friends. It would be a breach of protocol not to mourn."

"Humans have their own way of mourning. We should leave them to their ways, we wouldn't want to interfere with their customs."

"I'm surprised at you, Kevin. It would dishonorable..."

"It would be respectful..."

"It would be unheard of. Do it at once, and that's my final say. This is not open for discussion."

Without another word Kevin turned and left.

Even though escorted in together, the women still formed themselves into three groups. The Gorgons escorted them onto a raised platform turned and left rather quickly leaving the humans with no explanation as to why they were there.

This hold had a higher ceiling than most and they looked out over the lower floor, which was perfectly clean and empty.

Some thought they were going to be punished for something, some thought maybe this was the end of the mission. A few were terrified that they, too, would be flushed into space. Only one stood not caring about any of it, wishing he had something to sit on or a corner to curl up in so he could cry in peace.

Matt and Gary stood by their friend and the women stood behind them. Whatever it was, they would face it together.

At the far end of the hold a door opened. There was a low throbbing sound as Gorgons began to march in, all in perfect step. They marched in a straight line down one wall and with the precision of solders turned a right angle and marched across the room in front the raised platform the humans were standing on.

After fifteen had turned the next one turned behind them and as such slowly began to form a square. For the first time the humans noticed that none were wearing their coverings or had a ring on their hind legs, for all practical purposes they were naked. Without their coverings they all looked very much alike, there were only a few they could pick out if they absolutely had to.

The last Gorgon walked in but stopped just short of the end of the row. They were one short of a perfect fifteen by fifteen square.

Then, in unison, they turned and faced the front. Almost imperceptibly they started swaying. They swayed more and more until it looked like they would fall over then, on one big sway, they each took a step to the right.

As one.

The humans were mesmerized.

All the Gorgons then raised their hands and spun around. Eyes dropped to the outside, mouth stalks swung wide, arms raised and lowered, all in perfect step with each other as if they were locked together somehow.

The dance was beautiful. Now that the humans realized what was going on many shed a tear or two, held on to one another, and some openly cried. The dance settled into a bobbing circling motion and then one by one, seemingly at random, the Gorgons stopped and faced the front. After a few moments the last Gorgon finished and the entire group dipped and then stood up straight. Without any cue that the humans could see they all turned and with the back row started marching out again, only this time one Gorgon broke ranks, said something to another, and came and stood at the base of the platform. It was Bob.

The Gorgon he spoke with ran ahead of the others and after a few moments returned with his cover and ring on and with a translator on his back. Now that he was dressed the others recognized him as Joe. Kevin came in just behind.

Joe handed Bob his cover and ring and after he had properly dressed he stepped up on the platform and held his eyes low.

"When we lose a friend or comrade, we mourn together as one. The dance represents our lives from birth to…" he paused and lowered his eyes just a bit more. "To the end. We all end in our own time so the dance finishes with each ending at his pace."

Joel was trying to control himself. He wanted to sob but he also wanted to show that he was a man. His face was doing all kinds of acrobats and his mouth twisted in so many ways that Bob thought something was wrong with it. Finally, after a few deep breaths he said, "That was beautiful Bob. It was one of the most beautiful things I ever…" Like a dam breaking he let out a groan and started crying again. He covered his face with his hands and turned his back to the rest. Gary put his arm around him and told him it was perfectly okay to let it all out.

Matt turned back towards Bob. "We each mourn individually," he was losing some tears as well, "and at our own pace. No two do it exactly the same."

Bob looked around at the all the women, some silent, some crying, many hugging each other. There was no bickering, no words.

. "To us," he said, "that is beautiful."

They all stood there for a few moments and Annie, with her baby and Parminder, was the first to leave. Melody and her sister nodded at Matt and slowly made their way back to their hold. Soon it was just the three men and three Gorgons, just as when they first met.

Bob turned towards Kevin. "Would you do me a favor and check on the status on the new permissions tree? I will bring everyone up to speed on what happened."

"Certainly." Kevin hurried out of the hold.

Bob pulled out his remote and shut all the doors and raised a small wall out of the floor. Joel stared at Bob's hand on the remote. He hated these things now and didn't trust them at all.

Bob and Joe leaned on one side of the wall and the three men leaned on the other.

"I have something rather important to discuss with you. I would have waited, but time is urgent."

Joel was still trying to pull himself together, wishing he had a kleenex or something. Rather unceremoniously he blew his nose into his sleeve. Matt and Gary tried not to notice, after all he could be cut some slack.

"What is it, Bob?"

He leaned forward, which didn't have the effect he wanted as his voice still came from the translator. "This is in strictest confidence. Understood?"

They all agreed it was understood.

"Well, as you could see, we are missing a crew member. I was looking for him before the accident but he didn't show up for the dance, which is unthinkable. If he were on this ship then he would have been here today."

Everyone nodded.

"John was our senior Gorgon. He is older and has more experience than all of us. But he's no longer on the ship."

"Was he in the hold?"

"No, I couldn't find him before the accident, as I said. And…" Bob looked at the exits again, "This is the part I want to keep secret, I think Kevin knows something. He didn't want the dance to take place. I think he knew it would expose John as being gone."

This took even Joe by surprise. "Kevin? Little Kevin from Oginor Prime?"

"Yes, I'm not sure why but records do show he spent some time with John before he disappeared. I don't know what to think of any of this."

Matt elbowed Gary in the side and raised his eyebrows at him. Gary took a deep breath.

"Okay," he said, "Since we are speaking in confidence, I have something that I'd like to discuss with you."

After a few more moments of silence Bob finally asked him what it was.

"Well, and don't take this the wrong way, but we found out that there is actually oxygen in the atmosphere here."

Bob looked at him. "No, there isn't."

"Yes, there is."

"No, there isn't any at all."

"Yes, there appears to be lots of it."

"But that's impossible. Our life support readouts show no oxygen at all."

"But we started a fire, and fire won't burn without oxygen."

Bob stood up straight. "But…"

"I can show you, if you don't believe me. I'll have to find the lighter first."

"Let's go to the nearest computer room. I can show you."

Gary and Matt exchanged glances. "Wait, do you mean to tell us you really believe there is no oxygen here?"

"Look, I'm heading up an important mission. I'm trying to save our people. Everything is by the book, as you would say. I have no reason to hide anything from you at all. If there is really oxygen here then I'd like to know why it's not showing up in the environmental lists. Trust me, I understand what you are saying about the fire, let's just go see what the computer says."

Joel cleared his throat. "I believe him. Bob's been nothing but honest with us."

"I most certainly have. Come with me to the computer room and I'll show you."

***

Ten women sat around the main kitchen table with Terry, who they had practically dragged in after them.

"In school," he was explaining, "Usually around the first or second year. It's a very easy dance but also very sacred. I've only done it with family myself, as I expect most here have."

Dr. Hitchens was speaking for the rest of Gary's group. "I'm just amazed at how in synch you all were. Especially for this being the first time you all did this together."

"It is something we take very seriously. And this would be the first time in our history it was done for someone other than a Gorgon. We are all feel so bad about what happened."

"She would have been honored, for sure. I wish there was a way we could send word to her family."

Terry lowered his eyes. "Oh, Bob would kill us if we tried anything like that. Besides, only freighters are going down now, which reminds me, I need any final lists you may have. We have to move quicker now that we lost so many."

"They're around here somewhere..."

"If I may…" Terry said, hesitantly, "I was wondering something."

"Shoot."

"Shoot? Oh, I see." Terry bobbed his eyes a little bit in an alien chuckle. "Well, I was just wondering. Joel's group and Matt's group don't seem to get along. And there isn't much mingling at all between all three groups."

"That's a can of worms. I'm a psychologist, Terry, I've spent my whole life studying people and the way they interact with each other. Joel's group was picked because they were beautiful, a trait many humans hold in very high regard. Everyone wants to be beautiful and beautiful people are sometimes even treated differently. One theory states that it has become a survival trait and it's built into our genome to be attracted to those who may produce the best offspring…"

"Just a moment, if I understand you correctly you are saying Joel picked the best, and they expect to be treated differently."

"In their eyes." Dr. Hitchens tried to find the right words. "Everyone has their own idea of what constitutes the best. I think many of us here would agree that excelling in your field of choice would make you better than some. Some argue that it's all an illusion, we are each the best at something and arbitrary measures are not a good thing to measure all humans by."

Terry shook his eyes. "And what does all this have to do with worms again? And what, exactly, are worms?"

Before Dr. Hitchens could clear up her can of worms remark Gary came through the door looking rather excited. He started to speak but spotted Terry and stopped himself. Looking over the ladies he pointed and said, "Dr. Collum, and Dr. Plaitte, can you come with me. Oh, and Dr. Young, you're a chemist, right?"

Dr. Axely-Young only got a "Yes, but..." out before Gary asked her to come with them as well.

Once out in the hallway he asked where the lighter was and then headed towards the hold with Matt's group, explaining along the way that Bob was going to show them how the life support worked.

"Finally, some action."

***

After discreetly picking up the lighter, Gary met up with Bob and the others and they made their way to a small room with a slanted counter full of computer screens and buttons and lights of every size and color. Even the walls had screens on them. Everyone but Joel looked around in amazement.

"This is one of our auxiliary control rooms." Explained Bob. "We can access almost every system from here and everything can be configured for whatever job needs to be done. I think the gravity guys must have been using this one because many of these are showing statistics for the gravity generators."

The three women tried to make even a bit of sense of any of the readouts but the alien script looked like a cross between Chinese and ancient cuneiform writing with some Arabic thrown in.

"Let me just pull up life support, I'm sure that's where the atmospheric composition would be." He tapped some areas of a screen and various lengths of script lit up before the screen changed and it looked eerily like someone tapping links on a web page.

"Just a moment…"

"Go here." Joe suggested, pointing at a blob of script.

"That will take me back to the main menu, I'm already in the sub systems."

"No, you're in the gravity subsystems yet, this menu is the subsystem main menu. You want the main system main menu which shows the sub menus."

"But you can access the sub menus directly from any menu by using slide five if you know the title of the sub menu you want."

"You aren't in the same sub menu."

"Isn't the life support sub menu in the same system menu as the gravity sub menu?"

"No, it's proprietary, so they keep it separate."

"Can't I access sub menus directly if I know the name?"

"That only works on civilian systems, this is a control system."

"Wait, I just saw it, what was the last main sub menu I was at, I didn't mean to go past it."

The humans rolled their eyes and waited as Bob and Joe searched through what was supposedly several layers of menus.

"There it is! Now I can call up the composition." He tapped the screen a few more times then pointed. "See? No oxygen."

Everyone leaned down and stared at the strange screen.

"Um," Dr. Collum said, "We can't read that at all."

Bob actually knocked his eyes together. "I'm so sorry, there isn't a translation entity for the main computer. Well, here is the list of the major gasses. There's nitrogen, argon, helium, hydrogen, neon, methane, which is odd. And I'm sure these are translating correctly because they are one for one translations. But even in the trace gases there is no oxygen. There is a trace amount of nitrogen dioxide, which has oxygen in it, but it looks like such a small trace as to be almost nonexistent."

Dr. Collum reached into her pocket and pulled out the lighter. "This would not light without oxygen." She lit it. "And this huge flame would not be possible without a lot of oxygen." Everyone stared at the flame as if they were moths.

After a few moments Bob said, "Great green coils!" and turned back to the computer. "Joe, do we have any independent sub systems that can detect gas? What about the pilots? Don't they carry something for planet trips?"

"Yes, but I think the gas alarms work independently, let me see if I can find one and pull up its monitor."

Both Gorgons started working on multiple screens, Joe going much faster than Bob. Suddenly Joe stopped and stared at one small screen. "Bob," he said so calmly that he caught everyone's attention. "I think you'd better have a look at this."

Bob leaned over to look at Joe's screen. "Is that even possible?"

"Apparently, it is. If the gravity guys hadn't adjusted the resolution of this monitor I would have never caught it."

"Joe," said Bob slowly, "I want every single subsystem checked, can you do that for me?"

"I'll need help, or it would take weeks."

Matt cleared his throat. Then cleared it again. Then, after seeing the aliens not responding to him finally said, "What's the issue?"

"Oh, come over here so Joe can work, and I'll show you."

They all gathered around a screen and looked at the strange symbols once again.

"Okay, this may take a bit to explain." Bob began. He tapped some symbols and adjusted a slider making the print on the screen extremely small. "When we write code there are two parts to every line. You can see down this side a break." Indeed every line had a small space which lined up neatly splitting all the characters on the screen into two sections. "This side is the actual code, the actual commands to the computer. This side is reserved for comments, further instructions, notes to other programmers, or could be just left blank for that matter. These characters on the end are naughts, or fillers." Towards the ends of the lines the humans could see the same character repeated over and over to the end of the screen.

"Now," Bob continued, "The ship's computer is a mainframe, it's huge. Over huge, so the programmers gave each line seventy three characters for the comments, way more than enough. Even the longest lines have only twenty or thirty and so the screen is usually adjusted like this." He zoomed in so that only about twenty characters past the space showed. "This is the way it's always been done. On personal computers, like the one that powers the translator or just ones that we carry around the memory is not so large, there are only sixty eight characters left for comments. What Joe found was this." Bob adjusted the screen again, zooming out until he was at the end of each line.

All the lines were perfectly aligned, except one block was slightly shorter than the rest.

"This subprogram is from a personal computer." Bob could hardly get the words out. "Someone took out the ship's subprogram and put in one from a personal computer, you can tell because all the lines are a bit shorter. I'm not a programmer so I can't tell what's been done, but this is unheard of."

"Um," Dr. Plaitte raised her hand a little. "What does that subprogram do?"

"It monitors the atmosphere. I am assuming this is why there is no oxygen listed in the readouts when there obviously is. Someone didn't want us to know this."

He backed away and straightened himself out. As the defacto leader of this ship he felt betrayed and dishonored at this discovery and he wondered why, with the fate of his entire race at stake, why anyone would want to endanger his ship? And how did they do it?

"Listen. I don't know what's going on, and I am greatly disturbed by this. I don't know who did this or why but we can't let on that we know. Please, don't say anything to anyone. Joe and I will see if anything else was changed and maybe bring in a programmer to see what the change here actually does."

It was Dr. Collum's turn to clear her throat. "Bob," she said carefully, "if someone doesn't want us to know about the oxygen then maybe something is up with the machine that was supposed to convert every cell in our body not to need it."

"That machine was designed by our very best scientists for this very mission. I can't see how there could be anything wrong with it."

"Please, Bob, I am asking you, nay, begging you, to allow us to dissect that machine. It's true that you have technological advances like artificial gravity and faster than light space travel, but this is something we know a little bit about. What if someone knew it wouldn't work so put oxygen in the air and then hid that fact?"

Bob paced the room twice, lowering his eyes in thought.

Joe turned around. "I think they are right. It wouldn't hurt to crack it open and take a peek. But not the installers, let's just get a circuitry expert from one of the craft bays. All the humans are on board now and the machines are in storage so no one would know."

Again Bob paced. "Joe, you keep looking through the programs. Dr. Plaitte, how would like a close look at some of our technology?"

"Would I? You betcha!"

33

Matt entered the men's hold and looked around for a few moments. It was quiet and deserted and dark. He plopped down on a big couch and swung his feet up. After all that had happened he just felt like having a few minutes to himself.

A few moments later, however, Joel came in wanting the same thing. He sat on the next couch and tried not to show any emotion.

Matt took a deep breath, he knew what he had to say but it's never easy.

"Hey," he said, "I know how you must feel, if you ever want to talk or just need a shoulder to cry on or anything you know I'm here for you."

Joel nodded slightly. "It's just that I've never had to deal with a death before. It's so unreal. Someone I was just starting to care about is never coming back. It's just kind of unreal, you know?"

"Death is part of life. I remember when my mom passed away and seeing my dad cry and cry, but the next day he got up and went out to feed the cows and tend the milker. He was a lot quieter, but life goes on. The world doesn't stop."

"Only we aren't even on a world anymore"

"Yeah, I guess."

The men fell silent for a while, each lost in their own thoughts.

***

Karen was also sitting on a couch with Becky, Amanda, and Parminder all sitting nearby. It was Becky who noticed the tears in her eyes.

"What's wrong, Karen?"

After a long pause Karen finally answer. "You know, I was at rock bottom. No rent money, no good job, no boyfriend. I was just walking when I saw people running and cars stopping. Some kid stepped off the curb and was killed, right there. The first thought to cross my mind was 'why wasn't it me?' I felt that some kid, barely starting out in life, dies, and here I am, all messed up, hopeless, worthless, and I am the one who survives. I would have traded places with him right then and there."

They all just sat there, staring at the floor.

Karen continued, "I started seeing death everywhere. In the news, on TV, and every time I wished it was me. It became overwhelming. I knew nobody cared. That's when I got good and wasted and took this really sharp knife I had…" She trailed off.

"Anyway, I almost didn't feel like that this time. I must be improving."

"Life is precious." Parminder said, quietly. "When you are in an ocean, each drop becomes less important, they are all part of a larger whole, so much larger that it's incomprehensible. But put that same drop in a small bowl, with just a few other drops, and then all become important. A drop gone from the ocean means little, a drop from a small bowl can change everything. That's what we are now, drops in a smaller bowl. We are all important to each other now. You see every drop, Karen, even in the ocean, that's a gift, not a burden."

After a long pause Becky spoke up. "I never thought about it but I think you are right, Par."

"Maybe we should go hang out with the other girls. Get to know them a bit." Karen said, then added, "Just in case."

***

Kevin stared out a window at a small blue dot and wondered how humans ever got so far. He sensed Terry coming in more than heard him and having him sit by his side helped he feel just a little bit better.

"Well," Terry began, in the Gorgon's low throbbing language, "The humans are all very quiet."

"It's so unfortunate. I feel bad, I sort of gave them permission to look around, I never thought anything could happen."

"Hey, it's not your fault, all the remotes had programming errors, there was no way you could have known."

They leaned on each other, taking in each other.

"Kevin, there is a lot talk going around. Something is up. If you knew anything you'd tell me, wouldn't you?"

"Of course I would. You mean more to me than anything."

They leaned a little harder.

34

Tatyana had been feeling like so much baggage when Dr. Plaitte asked her if she'd like to examine some of the alien's technology. While most of her background in computer engineering was in the implementation of designs and not in any kind of research or development she couldn't wait to see how the aliens implemented their technology. She had already tried unsuccessfully to take apart one of the remotes and her efforts to see something as simple as their door technology also ended in frustration.

The main issue was getting anything apart. The remotes seemed to be a solid chunk of plastic and there were no panels or seams or anything that could be pried open by any of the doors. Just getting something open would be of great interest to her.

Dr. Plaitte and Tatyana met with Carl, the Gorgon who had rescued Joel and quietly they made their way to a small room where two large, covered tables sat.

Carl had a long talk with Joe and understood what was going on and his curiosity was just as peaked as the two humans he had with him. He pushed a cart of tools from his own collection, a collection built up over years as a landing craft repair technician and the women couldn't help but notice the similarities between these alien tools and those that could be found in any garage on Earth.

Gary and some others wanted to come but it was decided that secrecy was key so a small party was selected and it was this party that currently stood by the first table.

"Now," said Carl, "These were made by one of the bidders and there are two Gorgons on board who work with the company that made this as the on-ship technicians. They were here in case anything happened to these devices. I don't know them very well, but they seem a bit clueless to me."

"How so?" asked Dr. Plaitte.

"Well, I don't think they even know how to prep the endpoints of a basic biometal growth pattern let alone know how to regrow a degenerate system fault."

"Um, sure."

Carl took one of the unfamiliar tools off the cart, it looked like a chrome banana with a disk inserted into one end and some buttons on the other.

"What does this do?" asked Tatyana.

At first Carl didn't realize what she asking, then realized he was working with beings that hadn't even invented a flowing plastic yet. He decided that he would proceed with step by step explanations to keep the questions at a minimum.

"Well," he started, "when we make a device like this it's sealed so the inside is free of contaminates and kept at a vacuum to prevent corrosion and malfunctions. This breaks the seal, like this."

He ran the tool around the rim of the lid that covered the table, as he did so a seam opened up around the entire diameter. "It's basically a smaller version of what makes our doors work, only we need to separate the material manually."

Once he finished he put the tool down and picked up another that looked suspiciously like a flat screw driver. He forced it in the newly created seam and started to pry.

"Um, this tool is used to pry the two halves apart. Some assistance, if you may." As he pried with one hand he forced his finger coils into the opening and started to lift, the women, picking up on his cues, did the same until the tool was no longer needed and all three were lifting the cover off of the lid.

The inside astounded the women. It looked very much like opening a pumpkin only instead of a yellow, stringy, seedy mess it was a blue, stringy, seedy mess.

"Careful, now, don't lift too fast." Said Carl. "Those are the circuits and if we lift to fast they'll snap and..." he trailed off and picked up a small rod from his cart. Holding it with one hand it expanded until it fit neatly between the top and bottom part of the split lid.

"It's okay to let go now." He added.

His eyestalks lowered and almost inserted themselves into the mess of circuitry. "I've never seen anything like this." He said, almost to himself.

Dr. Plaitte and Tatyana still had no idea what they were looking at.

Finally Tatyana found her voice. "Can you explain what we are looking at?"

Without taking his eyes off the circuitry he tried to explain. "Well, when we design something like this any connections that have to be made off-board are coded, and then a biometal is introduced, different ones depending on what's needed, and it grows to make the connections needed. So the board on the top up here needed connections on the bottom, but..."

He trailed off again and looked closer at the top of the lid. One eye looked briefly at the cart and he expertly picked up another tool that was flat like a screwdriver but had a curved shaft. He poked it at a corner and some of the stringy mess started to drop away.

The two women crowded in to see what was underneath and it looked almost like a drawing of a normal circuit board that most of Earth's technology is based on.

"This just can not be…" Carl muttered. "It's like…it's like…"

He stared some more. The women wanted to shake him and make him talk faster.

Again he glanced at the tray and then picked up a tool that looked like a putty knife. Instead of being slow and careful he made some huge swipes at the upper lid, cutting large portions of the stringy mess down, after a few moments it was all removed and grabbed his support stick with one hand and with the other threw the lid all the way over so it lay completely open.

"Look at that." Carl said excitedly. "Just look at what they did."

"What, exactly, did they do?" Dr. Plaitte asked.

Carl glanced at both women. "It's completely random. It's like someone took endpoints gel and just splattered it on the endboard. This isn't anything at all. It's…it's…well, it's completely fake. Completely."

The next few moments he excitedly opened the lower end of the table and scraped off more blue stringy mess. Then he opened up parts of the next table over. After a while it looked as if a big blue pumpkin had exploded all over the room.

"I'm so sorry." Said Carl after resting a moment, "I was really hoping to show you how we design things and put things together, but this isn't anything. I mean, it isn't anything at all. It's just simulated filler. These tables are complete and utter nothings." He went on and on about how incredible he thought this all was, how much money must have been spent on such a fraud, and everyone fell for it. He finally ended by picking up one last thing off his cart and speaking into it.

"Bob, you really, really have to come down here."

Bob must have been nearby awaiting such a request as he showed up almost immediately.

"What did you…" he started to say as he walked in but stopped dead in his tracks when he saw the blue mess in front of him. He picked up a random piece and stared at it.

"Holy bouncing bubbles!" he shouted, surprising the women. They weren't sure if what he said translated correctly. "What is this? It isn't even fake, it's just random scribbles."

After picking up some other pieces and making what the women could only assume were profanities he turned to Carl. "Not a word, not a word to anyone."

"Can I at least ask what's going on?"

"Someone is lying to someone about something and I'm not going to rest until I figure out who is lying to whom about what."

Carl glanced at the women and is eyes bobbed slightly. "Well, okay then." He turned and slowly left the room, pushing his cart in front of him.

Bob turned and left as well leaving the two women alone.

With only a glance one picked up a small piece of the lid and one picked up a small ball of the stringy blue biometal. Then they headed back to their hold.

35

Karen, Amanda, Becky, and Parminder slowly entered the hold under the gaze of other silent faces. It felt like entering a foreign country which was bad enough considering they were on an alien ship far above every country that ever existed.

Marie was the first one to break the awkward silence. "What can we do you for?"

"Well," said Karen, "We felt bad about what happened at the party and we just wanted you to know that that, well, that the opinions and ideals expressed by some are not the opinions and ideals held by all of us."

Parminder added, "We have assholes in our group." Just in case the point wasn't clear.

Marie and some others smiled. "Come on in. We were just making some dinner."

"Is this everyone?" Amanda asked. "Your group looks so small."

"Well, Melody is Matt's fiancé and she and her sister are always off somewhere. One of us was a baby, and, um, then there was Marisa." Marie led them in and introductions were made.

Isabel was wiping down a pan. "We haven't decided on anything yet, any ideas?"

"You know what?" said Tracy, who was sitting next to Isabel, "I really miss hamburgers. Can we just make some hamburgers?"

"Oh," Isabel's eyes lit up. "And I saw some corn on the cob, and some big pots."

Tracy smiled, "Let's have a cookout."

Karen also smiled. "You know, we should invite the brains over, too. Let's have a real mixer. The guys are all off somewhere and the Gorgons seem to be busy."

"Sounds good, anyone want to walk down with me?" Tracy stood up and headed towards the door.

***

"Knock, knock." Karen said as the door to the hold slid up. Gary and ten women were crowded around the main table and all were staring at the two women in the doorway. "Did we come at a bad time?"

Tatyana waved them over. "Not at all, come have a look at this."

Karen and Tracy walked over and looked at the blue mess on the table. "What is it?"

Tatyana stood up straight as if making an important announcement. "Alien wiring."

Karen nodded slowly. "Ooookay." Was all she could think of saying.

Tracy was also nodding slowly. "We were having a sort of cookout, was wondering if you guys would like to join us."

Captain White was the first to say, "Would we? Sure. I'm famished."

A general round of "me, too" went around the table, including Amber. Gary, who had been wanting to get Amber back into a social setting, nodded along with the rest. This was not lost on Karen.

"Girls only." She said wryly.

Dr. Collum stood up and with a nod towards Gary said, "Sounds great." Amber also nodded at Gary as she stood up and started to walk out.

Tatyana and a few other were still poking at the blue wires and didn't want to break away from further poking at it. "You guys go on, I want to keep looking at this."

"As do I." added Dr. Plaitte.

"As do I." added Gary, obviously mocking the fact that he wasn't invited. He waved his hand mockingly as well. "You guys go have your little shindig." He flashed a smile around to show he was actually okay with everything, lingering only a little on Amber.

**

Except for the smooth black floors and low ceilings and the subdued lighting and all the pallets of merchandise spreading out for hundreds of yards behind them, it really did seem like a cookout of sorts.

Dr. Collum and Dr. Axely-Young found themselves staring intently at Isabel frying burgers in a large skillet.

"How would no oxygen affect frying a hamburger?" Dr. Collum mused.

"Not sure." Dr. Axely-Young said, almost to herself. "I never thought to fry a burger in a vacuum. I wonder if I could get a grant for that."

Dr. Collum chuckled. "I'll bet you can now. I'll bet any of us can get a grant for anything."

Isabel raised an eyebrow. "Are you still trying to figure out the oxygen thingy? There are a lot of us who'd like to go home any time now."

The two doctors exchanged glances then looked around at the activity around them. This wasn't a very private setting, however they both leaned forward and lowered their voices.

"Don't let this get around, but..." Dr. Collum waited for some girls to walk by. "We know there is oxygen here."

Isabel's eyes got a tad larger and she stopped poking the burger in the pan.

"Technically," Dr Axely-Young added, "We can leave at any time. But seriously, mum's the word."

"Oh my god. Are you for real?"

Again the two doctors looked around. "Yes, but shhhh."

Isabel leaned towards them, "Does this mean we are going home?"

"No, but it means we can. We're still looking into things."

"How do you know all this?"

"Well," Dr. Collum started, "It's kind of a long story. But we talked with Bob and he was just as surprised as we were."

"Doesn't surprise me," said Isabel, flipping some burgers. "All the aliens seem clueless about many things."

Before Dr. Collum could respond Parminder came up and leaned into the little group. Her eyes were red. "Is it true? We CAN return to Earth?"

Both doctors glared at Isabel.

"Well, don't look at me, I was here the whole time." She said, going back to her cooking.

They turned back towards Parminder. "It means we can, it doesn't mean we'll be able to. We are still thousands of miles in orbit with no way down and there's still the little matter of the Gorgon's mission to consider." Dr. Axely-Young didn't think this was comforting to her.

Parminder smiled, just a little. "But at least there is hope." It almost came out as a question.

"Just remember," added Dr. Collum, "No one is to know about this, no one." She turned towards the rest of the women and became aware of all the conversations going on around her, then she turned back towards Parminder. "Well, I think it's time to get everyone on the same page. THEN no one is to know about this."

"Ladies, can I have your attention…" Dr. Collum said, trying to wrangle up all the groups.

She didn't notice Parminder picking up one of the remotes and slipping into the hallway.

36

Joe the Gorgon tapped nervously at a control console. He had just called Bob down and was wondering how to fix what he had found but programming wasn't really his strong talent. He could troubleshoot code other Gorgons had written but writing it out himself was another matter.

Bob entered the control room and Joe thought he looked weary. Gorgons could tell when other Gorgons had gone a while without uncoiling and Bob certainly looked that way.

"You found something else?" Even his voice sounded weary.

"Yes," said Joe, stepping back and showing Bob the screen. Just like with the life support code this block was a few characters shorter per line than all the other code around it.

After a few moments of staring at it Bob stepped back. "I have no idea what that is."

"It's just the escape pod sub-routine. Every cycle it counts the escape pods and verifies they are all there."

"So, what does the new code do?"

Joe fidgeted just a little. "This new block counts the escape pods and returns a hard count, regardless of what the count actually was."

"Some could be gone but this would report they are all there."

"Yes."

After a few moments of silence Bob spoke again. "And are any missing?"

Joe fidgeted a little bit more. "I am working on that. I'm not even sure how many there are supposed to be. I was writing my own code when you arrived. It basically does the same thing the other code does, that is, it sends a signal to the power port of the escape pod, and if there is power then it counts it. If it's dead then it's counted as used."

"How much longer do you need?"

"I think I'm ready now, I was just going over it to make sure I didn't make any mistakes."

Bob stretched his arms and legs a bit. "Well, go for it."

Joe started tapping on the screen again and more lines of code scrolled past. He tapped a bit more, glanced at Bob, and tapped one last time.

Several other screens changed colors and low throbbing tones went off. Joe's eyestalks went straight.

Bob's eyestalks lowered.

There was a long moment of silence while both Gorgons stared at the screen.

"Did what I think just happen just happen?"

"I…" Joe could barely speak. "I am not sure how that happened." He started to tap frantically at several screens. "Oh, oh…"

Joe began to physically change color. It was a natural Gorgon reaction to realizing you had just screwed up in a major way in front of someone of some importance and this screw up could potentially risk the lives of everyone on board. It didn't help him think any clearer. Then he spotted it.

"Oh, I'm so sorry. I'm so, so sorry. I sent the signal to port seven instead of port nine. Port nine is the secondary power port." His voice was getting weaker. "Port seven is the, um, the power to the launch port."

Bob very calmly tapped a screen which switched to a picture of stars. He moved it around and it only showed stars and, briefly, the Earth. Nothing else.

"Where did they go?"

Joe searched some more screens. "It seems they were programmed to jump back home. Or somewhere. In any case they are all jumped."

"In a few minutes hundreds of empty escape pods are going to jump out at Gorgon?"

"If that's where they were going, yes."

"And now we have no idea if any were missing or not."

"No, no we don't."

Very calmly, almost too calmly, Bob turned and walked out leaving Joe to his colors. He just couldn't feel anything anymore.

37

Parminder entered one of the window rooms and pushed the button that exposed the tiny sphere that was Earth. She sat down and made herself comfortable and tried to imagine that what she was looking at was real.

The whole human race was on that sphere, and somewhere was her husband. She swore to serve him, to honor him, to love him for as long as she would walk the Earth, it never occurred to her that she would one day be walking and not be on the Earth at all.

He was there, waiting, and that was all she could hope for.

Looking down she thumbed a button she had pushed before, only the last time she ended up crying for hours.

Suddenly, she pressed it. If she had thought about it at all she may not have, but this wasn't a time for thinking things through. After a few minutes the door opened and a familiar Gorgon walked in.

"Terry?" asked Parminder, she wasn't sure if she could tell them all apart with certainty.

"Yes." Terry recognized Parminder. Her dark skin and jet black hair set her apart from most of the other models in Joel's hold. He also could never forget her tearful question from her first night here.

"Terry, come sit with me."

Perplexed, Terry adjusted a seat and sat next to Parminder.

"I trust you, Terry. You've been nothing but kind and honest to me."

"But of course, you are our honored guests. If there's anything I can do…"

"Terry, I don't know if you know this or not, and I'm pretty sure I'm not supposed to be saying anything…"

"Yes?"

She paused, so many thoughts were going through her head, she was suddenly very scared. She decided to change her approach.

"Have you ever been in love, Terry?"

Terry pondered for a moment, he wasn't sure how that translated as it was a very deep question for a totally alien creature to ask him and a totally odd time to be asked it.

"Well, as a matter of fact, and I'm assuming this translated correctly, I find myself caring for someone a great deal more and more each day."

"And you would do anything for this person, wouldn't you?"

"I think I would. I would do more for this person than for anyone else, that much is certain."

Parminder nodded. "I love my husband dearly. I would move mountains for him were he just to ask."

Terry turned towards the Earth. "I think I know how you feel."

A small smile played with Parminder's face. "Terry, I know now that there is oxygen here. Our bodies weren't changed, I can return to the man I love."

Terry sat up straight. His eyes bobbed slightly then turned back towards Parminder. "I don't think that's true. It's part of our mission to…" Parminder held up her hand and even the alien Gorgon knew what that meant.

"I don't know how much of a secret it's supposed to be but I imagine by now all the humans know it. I know Bob at least knows it, he helped figure it out with some of Gary's group. I'm sure there are others. It was discovered this morning, one of the machines was torn apart and it doesn't do anything."

It took Terry a few moments to figure out what machine she was talking about. It took another few to sort out if he actually believed this or not. His bobbing and rotating eyes must have been noticed by Parminder.

"I know it's a lot to take in." she said. "To be honest, I'm not sure how much of it I believe myself, and perhaps it was wrong to tell you, but I really need an ally right now. Someone I can trust who will help me."

Terry was still trying to digest this information when she went on. "You are in love, you know how it feels to want to do anything for the person you care about. Think about that feeling now."

He did, he did know that feeling.

"Terry, I am asking you from the bottom of my heart, help me get home before this ship leaves."

Icy chills ran through Terry's coils. This woman clearly didn't want to be here, and the reason she wanted to go home was to be with someone she loved very dearly. So many thoughts were colliding in his brain coil that he couldn't pick one to work on.

"I…I can't promise anything. I wouldn't be able to do it alone and if things are as you say then there may be some on board I can't trust. I will really have to consider this carefully. And we should not say a word of this to anyone, especially the other humans. If one leaves they may all want to."

Parminder stayed calm and poised, she turned towards Terry and for a moment they just looked into each other's eyes. Each was so alien to the other, but also so similar.

"Terry, thank you for understanding. I will be eternally in your debt."

"We have a saying, there are no debts between friends."

38

Bob had walked for nearly an hour around the ship just looking at the walls and nodding a hello to anyone he passed. The remaining freighters were working overtime but only eight more holds had been filled, one with nothing but diapers per the women's request. The window for jumping to Halfway was approaching and so many things were going wrong.

He found himself in the human's area and could hear a lot of chatter from one of the holds, but had no desire to check it out. The door was open to Gary's group and he could see them inside looking at some biowire. Such a simple thing he took for granted and these people had yet to invent it.

Passing unnoticed he continued on and in a short time he came upon the men's hold where he paused for a moment. Joel was sitting on a couch just staring at the kitchen area and Matt was on another couch talking quietly to his fiancé while her sister sat curled up not far away.

Melody spotted him and waved him in and Bob felt it would be polite to at least stop in and say hello.

One of the Gorgon stools was just sitting in front of the couch, where it was being used as a table, but as it was clear Bob came in and sat down.

"We've filled a whole hold with nothing but diapers." He said, simply.

Joel looked at him. "So, we are still going through with it?"

"I'm not sure what else to do. We are still a dying race without you. If nothing else we learned a lot to pass on to the next ship. Oh, and just so you know, all the escape pods are gone."

Matt raised his eyebrows. "Come again?"

Bob was getting used to the human's weird phrases, or at least was learning what they meant in context.

"The escape pod program was also tampered with, and while we were trying to see why we, well, sort of launched them all."

"That's kind of scary to think about." Melody said. "I mean, why mess with the escape pods?"

"Whoever did this didn't mess with the pods themselves, just the program that counts them. I am assuming it was John. He is nowhere on the ship and may have left in a pod and was just covering his tracks."

"That sounds logical." Said Joel.

"Any idea why he would want to?" asked Melody.

"No idea at all. He was probably the most experienced of all of us. Did a lot exploring missions, rescued a giant mining freighter once, helped set up some deep space stations." Bob lowered his eyes. "I ran some of the supply ferries that went to those stations. A very quiet, stable life compared to John's. I was very surprised the day a government rep showed up with new orders. I was so excited that we found a way to make more food. Everyone was worried about it with the oceans dying and all. And humans, wow. You can survive anywhere and do anything. I couldn't wait to meet you all."

"Well, not anything." Joel said quietly.

"I did talk to the representatives of the company that made the machines we found to be fake. They had only just been hired when chosen for this mission. I believe that they believe the machines really worked. You should have seen the shape of their eyes when I showed them the disassembled machine. That just can't be faked. They are tearing into them now."

They were talking so quietly and it was so peaceful in the hold that Bob found himself nearly uncoiling. He didn't want to say what he was thinking. If the two reps were hired for this mission and tricked into thinking their cellular machines really worked then whoever is behind this must be really high up and must be able to wield a lot of power. What he couldn't figure out is why. If they wanted to trick the humans into thinking they couldn't leave there would have been much easier ways. They could have just told them they couldn't leave, why make them think all their cells were changed? And why do it in such a way where virtually everyone on the ship was tricked as well? And why Bob? Bob?

"Bob!" Matt's yelling finally woke him up. "Bob, you're coming apart!"

"Are you okay?" asked Melody. Even Kim was jolted from her nap and was staring wide-eyed at Bob.

"Oh, I'm terribly sorry, I haven't had rest in the longest time." Bob literally pulled himself together and stood up.

Only Joel didn't seemed surprised at all. He looked at Kim and Melody and said, "You should see them come out of their pipes."

"Speaking of pipes, I should get back to my quarters." Slightly embarrassed Bob headed towards the door.

39

After Joel had described how he saw uncoiled Gorgons coming out of large pipes that were apparently their living quarters things got quiet again. He idly looked at Kim, who had dozed off again and wondered if he could ask her out.

Reality smacked his brain like a steel hammer. He wasn't back on Earth playing the field, he was in an alien space ship with aliens, and a girl he was just making out with was flushed into space like so much trash. The group he brought aboard, the group that was supposed to be his group, wouldn't even talk to him. Gary was busy trying to prove they could return and there was Matt, right in front of him, with the love of his life curled up in his arms.

Joel felt very alone.

And very hungry.

Forcing himself up he looked at all the greasy pans on the table and basket full of trash then ducked into the cold storage and emerged with a side of bacon. After a few moments the bacon was crackling and popping and attracting other humans.

"You going to eat all that?" Matt said as he sat down.

"I suppose I could spare a square or two, but I may need an extra package." Joel nodded at Kim as she sat next to Matt.

"Oh, no, I was just going to cut up a melon."

Matt looked over his shoulder. "Melody is conked out. It's been a long day."

Joel poked at his pan. "I wonder where my car is. I should have put it on the list. Is today Saturday? I lost track. I think I had a date."

"Joel…"

"No, it's okay. I'm okay. I will be." He poked through all the clutter that was building up on the table and found some paper towels and folded a few on a plate. "Shit happens, you know. I date cheerleaders, I have 10 freaking models for crying out loud, and I end up making out with a fat chick from Nebraska…"

"What the hell difference does that make?"

"I don't even know. I don't even know what the hell is going on anymore."

Kim cleared her throat. "You liked her because she was fun, she brought something out in you. She accepted you the way you are."

Joel slammed his spatula down so hard it even surprised him. "And who I am? I'm a failure. I'm letting the Gorgons down, I'm letting myself down. I'm a big fat sexist pig." Tears were welling up and he couldn't see the pan anymore.

Kim shrugged. "You're not fat."

Joel could barely hold back a chuckle. "Dammit, don't make me laugh when I'm trying to feel like shit."

"And get a new pan," Matt said, "I think I saw a tear fall in there and it really grossed me right out. I mean, seriously."

The sudden noise had startled Melody from her sleep and she looked up at the table. Joel was shaking his head and Matt and Kim were laughing at something, albeit a little quietly. Kim nudged Matt in the side and he leaned over and bumped shoulders. Joel pointed his spatula at them but she couldn't make out what they were saying.

They're just having a snack, she thought. Maybe trying to cheer Joel up. Other thoughts crossed her mind but she quickly tried to staunch them.

This was not the time or the place, she thought, for jealousy to rear its ugly head, especially towards her own sister.

***

Terry walked down the hall like a Gorgon with a mission. He knew the smaller ships were stored on their own in two separate holds and two of these ships were scout ships. They were barely ever used and were usually parked on their own along the back wall. He could picture them sitting there, dark and still.

If anyone asked he would just smile and say and say he was busy. Nonsense, no one would see him down here. All the work was being done with the four remaining freighters and the smaller ships were already prepped for storage, their missions having been completed.

As he expected he didn't see a soul on his way down. The hold was dark and almost creepy, especially the wall that Terry knew opened into deep space, which should be locked down with extra security since the accident.

The two scout ships looked almost identical to the other ships but they were more rugged and had more sensors and cameras poking out of them. Hulls were thicker. The chairs had more padding.

It had been a long time since he had sat in the cockpit of one these ships but it was all coming back to him. He turned on the power, making sure the engines were all completely disengaged and accessed the ship's computer. After a few moments he had the external sensors online.

It only took a moment for him to see what he came here to see. The moment seeped into his coils and seemed to harden, freezing him to his chair.

Without thinking he powered down the ship and sat there in the darkness.

***

Karen, Amanda, and Becky headed back into their hold not sure if it was nap time or time to go to bed as they had lost track of day and night. It was decided they were all still thirsty and would have a nightcap regardless of what time it was. As they entered the hold they saw they weren't the only ones.

Around the big front table were Cindi and her friends laughing and pouring wine.

They waved the new arrivals over with half empty wine bottles.

Why not, thought Karen.

"Well, it looks like you gals are having a good time." She said as she sat down.

Cindi smiled in her general direction. "I'll admit to having a bit of a buzz on."

Amanda picked up an empty glass and held it out, "I wouldn't mind a buzz." It was promptly filled for her.

While not particularly liking the four girls sitting opposite of her, Karen filled a glass and took a sip. It was sweet and sparkling.

"I don't recall seeing wine before. Was this a request?"

Cindi nodded. "Yep. They just brought it on board. I thought we'd christen it."

Karen put her glass down and glanced at Cindi. She really did look beautiful in the little red dress she had on. "Is that new, too? I thought there were no dresses on board."

"Yes, but don't worry, there's plenty for you, too. We beauties stick together."

Amanda and Becky looked at Karen, expecting her to go off but there was a far off look in her eyes. "Is that a real ruby?" was all she said.

Cindi just smiled and raised her glass. "We are honored guests and we were asked if there was anything we wanted. I simply gave them a list of things I wanted."

Karen smiled. "I'm sure you'll be living a life of luxury on Halfway. Here's to finer things." She raised her glass.

Amanda looked at her. "But…" Karen raised her hand, cutting her off.

"To Halfway." She said sternly. "Where these women will live the life of luxury." She winked and nodded towards Cindi and her friends.

"Oh, yeah, to Halfway." Said Amanda, realizing the secret of the oxygen had yet to make its way down here. She pictured herself back on Earth, doing a talk show, while Cindi and company sat alone on a balcony somewhere realizing they were the only ones there.

40

Bob slowly woke up and although it wasn't the best of sleep he felt relaxed and refreshed. He kept picturing a sunny morning on Gorgon, walking through the rocks on the shore, when suddenly a hundred life pods of all shapes and sizes come raining down through the clouds.

He was sure they'd send a probe out to see what was going on. And a probe may pick up Earth transmissions on how 33 humans were abducted by flying saucers. At least the supply runs were still stealthy. They knew how to break into computer systems and adjust inventories so for the most part a few humans were just left scratching their heads.

A beep was heard and he wondered how many beeps he had slept through. Without looking at his console he pulled himself together and headed for his private nutrients. As one of the highest ranking senior staff he was lucky to have his own private soak.

Again, two more beeps, and a boop. He told the computer to mute his messages and let himself relax a bit. He felt as if it was going to be a long day.

After a bit he got out and dried off and was finally ready to meet his messages.

Several were blue. Something bad had happened.

Bob was relieved that they were all related to the same incident, which seemed to be that a freighter was damaged. How in the world do you damage a freighter? They were great solid hulking working vessels that almost never broke down, you almost had to fly one straight into a mountain to break it.

Opening one of the blue messages he read an incident report on how two of the pilots had managed to fly one of the freighters straight into a mountain.

Bob banged all four of his eyes together.

Most of the other messages were routine with the exception of one from Joe, asking to see him as soon as he woke up. Something urgent, but not urgent enough to wake him.

He tapped a message to Joe that he was awake and Joe answered back that he was on his way. Without waiting, Bob walked into the hallway.

Joe found him before he got very far.

"I found some interesting things." Joe said, after their hellos. "I did some background checking and guess who Kevin's father is."

Bob confessed that he didn't know and didn't feel like guessing.

"His father was Governor General Harry." Of course, Harry was just the translator's name given to Kevin's father, his Gorgon name would have been completely unintelligible to any human.

Bob actually stopped walking. G.G. Harry was known for pushing for more off-planet exploration and mining, and for preservation of the home planet. He died in office of a disease that deteriorates inner strands which usually strikes in old age. There had been several Governor Generals since then, of his province.

"And there's more. Kevin was given some research assignments early on, and guess who he served under?"

Bob once again indicated that he did not feel like guessing.

"John. John was his commanding officer for his first three duty cycles. And guess who recommended Kevin for this assignment?"

Bob started walking again, mulling all this over in his mind. John wasn't on board the ship anymore and most likely took an escape pod back to Gorgon. Where...where...

"He could have told them anything he wanted. He would have to tell them something. You can't just show up planetside in an escape pod from one of the most important missions ever and expect to go unnoticed." He looked at Joe. "Load up a transmission buoy and send it off. Wait, check its programming first, make sure those haven't been tampered with either, then fire it off."

"What do we do now?"

"We continue. Have you discovered anymore systems that have been tampered with?"

"Not yet, I have four guys working on it." Then he added, "In secret, of course."

"How are the humans doing?"

"Better, I think. They have been doing more ice breaking, on their own."

"Good, good."

Bob and Joe continued walking not knowing that at that very moment Terry was just finding out all the same things about Kevin.

***

Isabel the nurse led Rachel down to the Brain's hold. Rachel was still in a state of shock and was having a hard time of it and Isabel thought that since this is where all the action seemed to be then maybe it would help her get involved with something.

Rachel just felt she was trapped in some nightmare and couldn': get out. Every day she would wake up on her big comfy couch and roll over to see an endless row of pallets stacked with boxes surrounded by black walls and odd creatures.

Isabel sort of tcok her under her wing and tried to explain how exciting it all really is and how they're all friends now and how friends look out for each other.

It didn't help that at this particular moment two of these creatures were sitting at the table while some female scientists were learning the basics of a technology that was totally unknown to Earth.

Without interrupting Isabel and Rachel saddled up to the table and nodded a silent hello to the other women around them. A Gorgon name Carl was doing a demonstration of how their biometal grows into circuits.

He was really enjoying the attention.

"Now this is crude example. I'm applying the endpoints manually when normally a printing machine would be used." With a small brush he applied some silvery metallic material to a clear chunk of plastic he had brought with him. This was a standard classroom demonstration that teachers would give to first year students.

He continued on. "The biometal would normally be programmed by a computer for anything from a simple light circuit to a complex holographic display. Based on that it senses the endpoints and the paths it has to take to make the circuit it was asked to make. Then it grows there." While he was talking the blue lumps at the bottom of the display started growing towards the silvery dots he painted at the top of the display.

"The advantage is that you can build something, put the controls where you want them, paint the endpoints where you want them, and then the biometal just finds the best path. If there's an obstacle," he put one of his finger appendages on the board in front of a growing blue strand and the strand started to curve around it, "then it just avoids it, still knowing where it has to go."

Tatyana also put her finger on the board and watched the blue strand change direction again. "But how does it do it? What is the mechanism behind the growth? How does it sense?"

The two Gorgons exchanged glances. "Well," continued Carl, "it's a bio material. It's actually alive, but not really conscious. Sort of like a plant. It's trained to do what it does. Here's a bit a trivia, it's all essentially from a single organism, all biometal comes from the same source."

"Like a banana." Said Dr. Hitchens.

"I have no idea what that means." Carl replied, but he still continued. "These strands, as I said, are crude. In complex systems they can be almost too small to be seen with a naked eye and grow in bundles for strength. There's really no limit to the configurations it can come up with."

Tatyana was shaking her head. "I still have way more questions than I can possibly ask. How on earth was this developed? What happens if a strand breaks?"

"Oh, that's the beauty of it." Carl handed the board to the other Gorgon then with both hands stretched a strand till it broke. Both halves curled against the board then pulled itself into two straight pieces that grew towards each other and reconnected. When it was over there was no sign it had ever broke. "Imagine snapping a whole remote in half, putting the two halves together and every circuit reconnects. It's why so many of our systems are foolproof."

"May I?" Tatyana said, pointing at the board. She pulled a strand apart herself and before they could reconnect she put her finger between them. The blue strands simply curved around her finger and reconnected. "I've got to know how this works."

The other Gorgon finally spoke up. "Well, we don't exactly know every little detail, it's just something we use without question. It just works. Well, most of the time." He nudged Carl and his eyes started bobbing slightly.

"Oh, hush."

"Go on, tell them Carl."

Tatyana looked at the two. "Tell us what?"

"Well, okay, but this is embarrassing. Really embarrassing." Carl's eyes drooped just a little while the other Gorgon's eyes kept bobbing. He seemed to enjoy putting Carl on the spot.

"I was working in a huge entertainment complex. It was state of the art, holograms, information booths, shows, well, it had everything. All the walls and displays were in place and the endpoint printers had just inserted most of the endpoints and the computers had programmed the biometal. I was carrying two casks of this endpoint appliqué when one of the lids came loose. I didn't know it but I had dripped from one end of the compound to the other."

"I can only imagine." The other Gorgon's translated voice almost seemed to be laughing.

Carl grudgingly continued. "Well, even though the biometal was programmed it sensed the extra endpoints and tried to include it into its circuitry. Biometal filled the main hallway, the reception area, and the path to the parking lot.

Every component malfunctioned, printed endpoints shorted out..."

Still sounding like it was laughing the other Gorgon cut in. "I heard holograms were being projected everywhere, the whole entertainment program got mixed into the control programs so nothing could be controlled and computer terminals were putting on shows. It set the whole project back months."

The women standing around could only manage a few chuckles. It sounded mortifying for poor Carl.

"Can you imagine flipping the lights on but instead being greeted with a nutrient fountain singing a chorus?"

Carl's eyes bobbed slightly. "Okay, it was a little funny."

Isabel nudged Rachel and whispered, "See? Even aliens screw up, just like us."

Captain White, who was standing next to Rachel couldn't help but overhear.

A few feet away Gary sat on his own and quietly listened to the whole conversation. He was daydreaming how biometal would change the history of the world when he spotted Amber leaving the table with a drink and sitting down on her own, lost in her own thoughts. He couldn't resist and followed her over.

Sitting down he said, "So, what do you think of biometal?"

"It's…really cool, I guess." She was slightly annoyed at Gary's presence but knew it was probably something that couldn't be helped. "I mean, can you imagine building a house and you just have a clump in your basement then you stick a lamp on the wall where ever you want it and it just grows a connection and poof! You have a light."

"Oh, more than that." Said Gary. "Imagine putting a big clump on Hoover Dam and it just grows to all the houses. Underground even, where it's perfectly safe an out of the way. And if some guy is digging a ditch and cuts a strand, it just grows back."

"Yeah, sure." Amber nodded, sipping her juice.

Just then Captain White walked up and smiled slightly. "Gary, can I have a word with you?"

Every single time, thought Gary. I'll never get to talk to Amber alone, but all he said was, "Sure."

Captain White sat down, not minding that Amber was there as well. "There's something really bothering me about this mission."

"Which mission?" asked Gary.

"The Gorgon's mission. I've talked with several Gorgons about why they're here, and heard other stories. They are all screw ups, for lack of a better term."

"How do you mean?"

"Well, look at this guy, ruined a huge entertainment complex. One guy accidently poisoned his ship's food supply, one blew up half a moon, one sent two robotic freighters to the same place at the same time and they destroyed each other. The list goes on. And what's more is what's happened since we've been here. All the doors were programmed wrong. They are supposed to be secret and stealthy yet they stormed a hospital in broad daylight to kidnap a baby and every news channel on Earth is buzzing about aliens. And, in spite of all their technology, two pilots managed to fly right into a mountain. Do these seem like the kind of people you put in charge of saving your entire planet?"

Gary mulled this over in his mind.

Captain White continued. "Think about it. The most important mission in history, wouldn't you send the best of the best? What kind of mission do you send the worst of the worst on?"

Again, Gary thought about this.

"A mission doomed to failure, that's what. From what I can tell there was only one Gorgon on this whole ship who had an impeccable record and you heard what happened to him."

Before Gary could answer Captain White finished. "He abandoned the ship."

41

With his eyes held high Bob marched through the corridors of the ship with an air of confidence and importance. Something very strange was going on and it would be up to him to make sure this mission went as planned. He was cut off, alone, and was willing to do whatever it took to deliver his cargo to Halfway.

Bob felt so confident that when Tom came around the corner with his low ring on that hind leg he said, "Good morning, Tom, you sexy, sexy thing."

Tom nearly uncoiled as Bob just strutted past.

Rounding several more corners he finally reached the control room where Joe's computer experts were going through every program on the ship. As the door went up he was surprised to see two Gorgons heatedly yelling at each other.

"Hello, what's...hello, HEY." It took Bob a moment to get their attention. "What's going on here?"

A Gorgon called Pete turned around, visibly shaken. "Bob..." he started.

Much of the confidence Bob had been feeling decided to melt away at that point.

He looked at the screen the two had been working on and saw the tell tale signs that it had been tampered with. "What program is that?" he asked, cautiously.

Pete exchanged glances with the other Gorgon. "It's navigation, Bob. It's the navigation program to Halfway. The whole thing. Without the NavCom from Gorgon, well..."

Bob knew what he meant. Faster than light interstellar travel was horrendously complicated and dangerous. It took tremendous computer power, more than almost any ship had so to facilitate things a main computer had been built on Gorgon and navigation routes were laid out there and transferred to ships leaving the system. Like electronic templates each route could then just be plugged in. Unplanned faster than light was out of the question and only probes went in directions not pre-planned by the NavCom.

Most of those probes were never heard from again.

With all this running through his mind all Bob could say was, "Explain."

"Bob," Pete said carefully, "All the backups are gone. The scheduled backups were stopped when we launched. This is the only navigation program left in the computer. And we have no idea where it goes."

Bob searched his mind for anything that made sense. "There's no escape pod navigation or probe navigation we can plug in?"

Pete's eyes circled a no. "The pods carried their own and they're all gone. The entire communication buoy's programs are all corrupted as well, but in a different way. We have no idea where they're going. Plus they are proprietary so we'd have to convert them anyway, and that would take weeks."

Pete's last words shook the last of Bob's confidence that he was actually in charge. "Where ever this ship is going, it's going there blindly."

This was too much. Raising his remote Bob pressed the buttons for a ship wide announcement.

"Attention everyone. I need all senior staff to meet in the auditorium in half an hour. This will be an open meeting and I would like everyone who can to be in attendance. To all humans, this is of great concern to you as well, I need you all there as well." He started to put his remote down but then added, "And I want you all to behave."

***

Three men sat around the kitchen are nibbling on bacon and contemplating what Gary had just said.

"Why would they want this mission to fail? What would that accomplish?" Matt could hardly wrap his head around the concept.

"Bob seems to believe in it. The crew seems to believe in it. It seems logical given the story they gave us. The only thing I would question is taking people secretly instead of asking for volunteers." Joel stared off into the dark hold. "Maybe all Gorgons are like this. Maybe this is the cream of the crop."

Bob's announcement filled the air. All three men got an uneasy, sinking feeling in their guts.

"Half an hour, I'd better wake Melody." Matt said.

"Why is she sleeping so long?"

Matt paused and finished his milk. "Well," he said sheepishly, "we were up arguing all night long. It seems she thinks I'm attracted to her sister."

Gary and Joel raised their eyebrows and looked everywhere but at Matt.

"Hmm." Joel took a breath. "If only someone had warned you about that."

"Oh, shut up. You know and I know I was just trying to keep her happy. I have no interest in her sister at all. I just thought she wanted family…"

Joel raised his hand. "We're talking about women here, and appearances, and emotions, and a very unique situation."

Matt nodded vigorously. "That's what I tried to tell her, it's just appearances, and I was kinda on the spot about picking women. I did bring Annie's baby on board, that should show what a nice guy I am."

Shaking his head, Joel just replied, "Nice guys finish last."

"Ugh, I am not getting into this particular conversation." Gary popped one last bit of bacon in his mouth and headed towards the door.

***

Karen stared in wonder as Cindi and her friends scrambled to get ready on such short notice. It's not that they were overdressing, but even this level of preparation was overkill for whatever meeting Bob was thinking of.

She couldn't hold her tongue any longer. "This isn't a job interview. What's all the fuss about?"

Cindi rolled her eyes. "I strive to look and be my best regardless. If I show up dressed in…well, in sweats or something then people will think I don't try or that I don't care about how I look. If I don't care about how I look then how can I care about other things? People will lose confidence in me."

"Nobody here even knows you, no one has confidence in you to begin with."

"All the more reason to look my best. Then they'll know I have pride in my appearance, and by extension pride in all aspects of my life."

Karen shook her head. "You way over think things. No one is going to look twice at you, except maybe Joel."

"People respect people who take pride in their appearance. It's the extra effort, it's going the extra mile. If someone needs someone to get something done are they going to ask a brawn in a house dress or someone who took the time to iron her clothes and who can hold their head up high?"

Parminder, who had been listening, came up and sat next to Karen. "There is nothing wrong with looking your best." She said.

"Thank you." Cindi said, with some satisfaction.

"As long as it is not for vanity's sake."

Cindi rolled her eyes again. "I'm not vain. I just know how to get things done."

"How to get what you want, there's a difference." Karen said.

"It's how the world works." Cindi snapped. "I don't make the rules I just play by them. And yes, I play to win, there's nothing wrong with that."

Karen looked at Parminder. "Well? Is there anything wrong with that?"

"No." Karen looked half surprised. Parminder went on. "We each follow our own paths. Cindi seems very happy on the path she's chosen. I was happy on mine until I was abducted. As long as she is not hurting anyone I wish her the best. It is very hard to find true happiness by watching where others are going. I choose my steps carefully, and go where I want to go, where I must go."

Karen looked down, she still thought Cindi was a materialistic snob but perhaps Parminder was right. Maybe she should mind her own business. She looked back at Parminder.

"So the way she keeps calling Matt's group the brawns doesn't bother you? The way she belittles and mocks them?"

Parminder shook her head slightly. "It is not a word I would use, and it is not an attitude I would have. I think she knows I disapprove, but it is not my job to change her. Does it bother me? Maybe a little, but I take comfort in knowing that I do what I believe is right, and that she has the freedom to do what she believes is right."

"Well, she shouldn't insult them right to their faces."

"On that we agree."

"Look," said Cindi, "I'll leave them alone if they leave me alone. Just try to remember who started what the other night. I didn't walk in on their conversation and throw insults around, she walked in on mine. Like Par said, if she doesn't like me, that's fine with me, just stay out of my way."

"I don't get any of you." Karen stood up and headed towards the door. "We're all in the same boat. We should be pulling together, not staying out of each other's way."

42

Bob set the room up personally. He raised what looked like church pews in three sections for the humans and between each section he raised the stools that Gorgons preferred. On the stage he raised a large oval table with stools around it and placed translators on the table and made sure the whole room could hear everything.

Matt and Gary arrived first and eyed the seating arrangement and without a word Gary sat in the middle section and Matt took a side. Some Gorgons were already arriving and sitting randomly around.

Joe and Tom came in and sat at the table, and then Kevin. With all that was going on Bob almost forgot that Kevin was senior staff and still had many responsibilities aboard the ship.

All the women started to file in and without question sat in separate sections and looked silently at each other. Joel came in last and while crossing in front of his group Karen motioned him over.

"Sit by me." She said. He looked around and although he saw Cindi roll her eyes he decided to take the invitation. "I've been thinking," Karen continued as he sat down. "We haven't given you a chance to say anything and we do feel really bad about what happened. And, well, this seems like an official meeting so just sit here."

Joel sat at the end of the bench and glanced over at the ten models. For once they just seemed like normal women, sitting normally, in an alien theater, surrounded by aliens.

Terry came in and sat down next to Kevin. He handed him a personal pad and said, "Here, you left this in a control room. You should be more careful."

"Thank you," Kevin said. "What would I do without you looking out for me?"

"Is something wrong? You seem distracted."

All the escape pods are gone, he thought, but only said, "Nothing much, just wondering what all this is about."

When the room and table were full Bob stood up which silenced all the Gorgons. It took a moment for all the humans to be silent as well.

Bob paced in front of the table.

"There have been some developments." He started, with his voice being projected all over the room and the rest of the ship for those who couldn't attend. "I know there are rumors flying around both with the Gorgons and the Humans. I'd like to take this opportunity to fill everyone in on what's going on so everyone has the most up to date information."

Bob paused to collect his thoughts. This had to be done.

He carried on. "John, one of our most experienced leaders, has disappeared. We believe he used an escape pod to return to Gorgon. The reason we believe this is that our escape pod subroutines have been corrupted but in our attempt to repair it, um, all the escape pods were inadvertently launched so while we can't confirm he left in a pod, we have every reason to expect he did." Then he added, "Also, don't screw anything up, we have no escape pods."

Terry fixed his eyes on Kevin, at the mention of escape pods he seemed more saddened than surprised.

Joe raised his hand and it took a moment for Bob to see it, when he did he gave Joe the floor.

"Bob," he started. "We now know that John is back on Gorgon. We got a reply to the information buoy we sent."

"Well, read it."

"Here? In front of everyone?" Bob waved his hand and Joe picked up a pad from the table and read. "Bob and the crew of Tub. I have received your message and have passed it on the council. As you are probably aware I had to return unexpectedly and since I've been back I had the Gorgon Council appoint me the liaison for this mission so any future buoys will come directly to me. I am glad to report to the council that everything is going according to plan. I am sorry to see all the escape pods come back empty but was able to divert them to avoid any panic on this end. I look forward to hearing from your successful landing at Halfway."

After a long pause Joe added, "All the buoy's homing programs have been altered. We think it was John's plan all along that he intercept all incoming buoys. We could report the Earth has blown up and he could report to the council that things were going as planned."

A low murmur went through the Gorgons. Many were still out of the loop and they were left piecing together the information coming at them.

Bob paced the floor twice. Almost the entire crew of the tub and all the humans watched him intently.

"Which brings me to my second point. The navigation program that we were to use to travel to Halfway has been tampered with. As of this moment we have no idea where we are going."

The entire room gasped except one. While everyone started talking at once Terry watched as Kevin made no reaction to this news. As far as Terry was concerned this was the last piece of the puzzle. Bob also watched as Kevin just stared at the table.

Bob held his hands up and the room once again fell silent. "Just before this meeting we discovered one last thing. As you all know, once the drives start gearing up for launch they are nearly impossible to shut down." He took a few steps. "The emergency disengage programs have been erased from the computer."

From the next outburst the humans could deduce what this meant. The ship was leaving whether they wanted to or not.

Tatiana raised her hand. "Why can't the drive be shut off?"

Joe stood up. "I know you humans haven't developed faster than light travel yet but the drive has to build up momentum. If you try and stop that it can fly apart, along with any ship it's attached to."

For most of Gary's group this was just another teaser into the mechanics behind faster than light travel, but they let it go in light of the more serious issue of what was to be done now.

Terry continued to stare at Kevin. A stranger was sitting next to him. Where was the Kevin he knew and loved? Where was the Kevin he trusted? He couldn't hold it in any longer.

"Bob."

Bob turned around and was surprised that Terry had spoken up. "What is it, Terry?"

Terry looked at the pad in front of Kevin. "Bob, what does Halfway look like?"

The question caught Bob off guard. "What do you mean?"

Terry shrugged. "What does Halfway look like?"

Bob glanced around at all the Gorgons and Humans sitting around him. "Well, I've never been there but where we are going to land it's forested, with a rocky coastline..."

"No," Terry interrupted. "I mean the whole planet, what does it look like?"

Kevin nervously pulled his pad to him and became tense.

"Well," started Bob again, "it has two large continents that are mostly dessert and because of its tilt it has one large polar cap and one small polar cap. Between the continents are a few small islands that are heavily forested. Why do you want to know this Terry?"

Terry watched as Kevin tapped idly on his pad. "What planet has five smaller continents and two small polar caps? Almost all evenly spaced?"

Bob thought for a moment. That sounded really familiar but he couldn't place it. Again he asked Terry why he was asking this.

Terry looked directly at Kevin who was bobbing his eyes in the universal Gorgon body language of "no".

"I saw projections. Population projections for human expansion. Only the planet wasn't Halfway. It wasn't two large continents."

Kevin backed off his stool, staring intently at Terry. "Why are you doing this to me?" he stammered.

Terry stood up. "You knew there was oxygen here. Tell them, Kevin. Tell them what I saw."

Kevin threw his pad on the table. "You saw nothing. It was just normal projections."

Terry picked up the pad and looked at it in horror. All doubt was now gone. "This has been erased." He said. "You just erased your pad. Just now."

Kevin backed up more. "I did it for us, Terry. I had a pod ready for us, I had no idea that they were all going to be lost. John had set us up for life. I did it because I love you…"

"YOU LOVE ME?" Terry screamed. All the Gorgons sitting at the table slid off their stools and backed away. "You love me? What was on that pad, Kevin? What in the name of the four corners was I looking at?"

"The Minks." Bob said. "I remember now, we only ever saw it once when the first probe was shot down. That is the Mink homeworld."

Kevin's eyes were darting around faster and faster and he took a few more steps back. "Well, why not?" he shouted back. "They did it to us, we were just going to do it back to them."

"Do WHAT?" Terry took another step towards him.

"Well, look at them." Kevin pointed at the humans. "Do you know creatures lived on their planet for millions of years? Hundreds of millions! But they all stayed in the same places, doing the same things. Then all of sudden they get wiped out, and other creatures emerged." His eyes kept darting. Even through the translator his voice was cracking and practically screaming. "Then they came along. Humans. In the shortest time they were everywhere. Mountains, deserts, forests, oceans, even at the poles. Then they multiplied, growing into the billions, consuming everything."

Kevin's voice grew angry. "And that was when they were primitive. Look at them now. They took over their holds, they were crawling all over the ship like...like..."

"Like cockroaches." Gary was surprised that his voice was projected all over the room.

"You're sending us to Mink to breed like cockroaches."

Kevin was nearly against the back wall. "They launched a biological weapon at us, we are just launching one back. The council rejected this plan in favor of Halfway. They are blind to what this means. In a few centuries humans will replace the Minks and the threat will be gone. We are doing this on our own."

"Who is we, Kevin? For it sure as hell isn't us." Terry's eyes were as high as he could lift them and his voice was so full of anger that everyone was backing off.

"John, and the Governor, and me, and the fleet commander, and others. We did what the council wouldn't do."

"Don't you realize what you've done? You've doomed us all. You said you loved me and you've doomed me to die on Mink. Is this how you freaking love me?"

Kevin couldn't take any more and bolted towards the door with Terry right on his third heel. Joe started after them but Bob jumped in his way.

"Let them go. It's all out in the open now and there's no where Kevin can go." Bob lowered his eyes as nearly 200 Gorgons started to panic. "Whatever Terry does to him will be more punishment than I can give."

Bob turned towards the rising crowd and waved his hands. "Please, everyone sit down and be quiet. Please."

All the Gorgons seemed to obey almost immediately leaving the humans to their murmuring. The last thing anyone said was, "I don't want to die a virgin."

All the humans fell silent and stared at Joel, who was instantly shocked that his voice was projected around the room. He sat down wide eyed and staring at the floor, turning a color red that surprised the nearby Gorgons.

Cindi took a few steps forward. "Do you mean to tell me you put us through all this and you're a fucking virgin?"

Somewhere someone started to giggle. Then another, then another. Within seconds all the humans were howling with laughter.

"Bob, they're doing that thing again." Said Joe.

Joel started to shout. "Will you all lay the hell off of me? This is serious." His voice was nearly drowned out. "We have to figure out what we are going to do. Will you all just stop it?"

He was nearly in tears.

"ALLRIGHT! THAT'S ENOUGH!" Bob's voice was so loud that the humans were shocked into silence. They all sat down red faced and breathing hard.

Bob turned towards Joe. "Is there any way to stop the countdown and spin up to light speed?"

Joe waved his hand. "We can shut it down manually if we, no wait, it's too late for that."

Bob paced again. "What if we remove the navigation program? We did that once on a freighter."

Joe thought about this. "Well, maybe. I know about that trick but have never tried it myself. Let me go look." He darted towards the door.

Tatiana jumped up. "Can we go?"

Bob waved his arms. "I don't see why not at this stage."

Tatiana ran after Joe followed by Captain White and Dr. Plaitte.

Bob looked at the sea of eyes and human faces staring at him.

"This is the last time I call a meeting." He muttered.

Matt stood up. "Bob, what do we do now?"

Bob paced one more time. "Well, let's see if we can trick the engines into shutting down. We have plenty of time to get you," he looked at all the women and the three men he had come to know so well, "all of you, back down to the planet's surface. I think it's safe to say this mission is over. We have failed. We have been sabotaged." His eyes hung down and all the Gorgons felt bad for him. Again he looked at the sea of faces. "Regardless of what happens to this ship, you are going home."

43

Joe entered a control room followed by three humans he knew had no idea what was going on. He sat down at the biggest screen and could feel all six eyes looking over where his shoulders would be if he had any.

Dr. Plaitte was the first to speak. "So, how does faster than light travel work to begin with? What, exactly, is spinning up?"

Joe knew this question was coming but still wasn't sure on where to start. "Well, space has gravity wells and at the bottom of each well is a mass. I'm not sure how this is translating."

"So far, so good."

"And we generate a well in the center of the ship and it slides us towards our destination, but we have to avoid any wells between where we are and where we want to go."

"But how does that work? How do you achieve the sliding towards the destination?"

"Well, I'm not really sure. It's all proprietary and the company that makes them are loath to give out their secrets. It's the program itself I'm concerned with right now."

"So what are you doing to the program?" Tatianna asked.

"Well, the program is built in modules that are linked with code. The trick Bob was talking about is to take out the actual launch and navigation program and link the spin up portion with the arrival program and if it works then that tricks the computer into thinking it completed the journey and starts the spin down."

"And if it doesn't work?"

"Then we'll all be part of a brilliant explosion that I'm sure your people will talk about for generations to come."

Captain White sat back, "Well, that's comforting. Maybe we should evacuate the ship before you try this."

"We'd love to, but if this isn't done in the next few minutes then this ship is leaving for Mink in a few hours. If it leaves while there are freighters in the air then their computer uplink will be broke and they'll all be flying into mountains."

The three women stared as strange symbols scrolled across the screen faster than they could make any out.

"This is going to take time." Joe muttered. "Too much time, I'm not sure I'm going to make it. I'm not sure I can do this at all." Joe's eyes started to sag.

Tatianna leaned forward. "Joe," she said, and the sound of his name coming through the translator really caught his attention. "Everyone on this ship is counting on you, and for no other reason than they trust and believe in you. They know you can do this and so do we. The real trick is having that same trust and belief in yourself. Do your best, that's all we ask."

Joe stared at the screen. This level of programming was not something he delved into very often but it was familiar and each line he understood gave him that much more confidence.

"Yes, yes, I can do this."

The three women backed off knowing that there was really nothing they could help with and any further questions would just be a distraction.

Outside of the room stood Bob who had heard the whole exchange. There was something in the way the humans gave Joe confidence that amazed him. They somehow made him a better programmer with just a few words then let him go.

In spite of Kevin and Joe and the conspiracy against them, he was very proud of his crew, he just hoped he lived long enough to tell them that.

***

Back in the meeting hall twenty-six women and a baby gathered around the three men who had brought them there. Many of the Gorgons still lined the walls just idly listening and watching to see what the humans would do next.

"Alright, everyone listen up." Matt was trying to get the women to quiet down but talk about how famous they were about to become was hard to stop. He even heard mentions of what kind of lawyers to get and where to find a good agent.

"Everyone, if you could just listen up…"

Isabel the nurse pushed her way up front. She smiled and nodded at Matt then turned around.

"HEY!" she shouted with such force that not only did all the women stop talking but half the Gorgons in the room nearly uncoiled. "Let's listen to what Matt has to say."

Matt nodded slightly and cleared his throat. "Thank you, Isabel. Now, everyone needs to go back to their holds and prepare to leave. Stay together so we know where to find you at a moment's notice. And I just want to say it's been a pleasure to meet each and every one of you."

There was a general murmur of agreement, although some was very reluctant.

Parminder smiled for all to see. "Soon I will be with the man I love."

Dr. Collum shrugged. "I still don't know how artificial gravity works. But the living wires will keep me busy for years."

Gary grinned. "Well, I know that whatever happens, at least I'm not a virgin."

As laughter erupted and Joel started punching Gary's arm a very smooth vibration went through the ship. So smooth that only the Gorgons who were watching the humans with curiosity noticed it.

The humans also didn't notice the Gorgons exchanging alarmed glances.

***

"Kevin!" Terry yelled. Without translators the yell was low and throbbing and desperate. The hold was dark and quiet and Terry listened intently, trying to hear a footstep or anything that would tell him what direction to look in.

Conflicting emotions tumble around inside him, sending zinging sensations up and down his strands. On the one hand he loved Kevin and wanted to keep him safe, on the other hand he wanted to rip his eyes off and shove them up his strands.

"Kevin, come out so we can talk. You know there's nowhere to go and no one is coming after us. It's just us. It's just you and me."

In the distance he heard a slight bloop. Terry tried to home in on it and felt bad that Kevin was so upset that he was blooping. He looked at the idle trays of tools that were left around and spotted a mechanic's helper. That would do the trick.

He put it up to his eyes and looked around. The nearest ships became transparent revealing the wires and framework inside, but there was no sign of life. He twisted the range knob and as the nearest ships became solid again the furthest ones faded revealing a red outline of Kevin crouched along the far wall. It appeared he was looking at a tool bench himself.

Terry set the mechanic's helper down and quietly walked through dim hold. What should he say? How should he act?

He rounded the last ship and when he saw what Kevin had his eyestalks stood up straight.

"Kevin," he said quietly. "What are you doing?"

Kevin could barely talk. "Everything is ruined. I can't face anyone."

"You can face me."

"No. No, I can't."

Indeed, Kevin kept his gaze fixed on the tool in his hand.

Terry took a few steps forward. "I thought we got rid of all of those." He said calmly.

A red line came out of the front of the shiny tool, just barely touched the floor, and then snaked back up where it curled several times around Kevin's midsection.

"I can't face anyone. I betrayed…" He could barely hold his eyes up

"Kevin, we can work this out. Do you really want to leave me like this? I thought we had a future together."

"Had. There is no future now."

The tool drooped lower, but Kevin's hand was still on the activation lever. Terry took a few more steps towards him. Just a few more and he might be able to grab the safety before Kevin could act.

He just had to keep him talking. "Listen, when we get back and expose all of this you can be exonerated…"

Kevin drooped even more and some of his coils were falling loose. "There is no going back. This ship is going to Mink."

One eye stalk barely lifted. "Terry…"

"I'm right here, Kevin."

"I love you."

The red line effortlessly coiled back into the tool that controlled it making those the last words Kevin would ever say.

Terry fell to the floor, howling. What he just saw pushed all thoughts from his head and replaced them with stinging pain. After several long moments of sheer hopelessness he gathered himself up one more time. It took everything he had to reach out.

And pick up the tool out of Kevin's motionless hands.

44

Gary rubbed his arm as he walked down the hall with the other humans. In a pinch, Joel sure could hit hard, but it's not something he cared to admit right now.

Down the hall ahead of him he saw Amber turn away from the others and go through a door to one of the window rooms. Now was his chance.

As he entered he found her already pressed against the glass, looking at the tiny blue marble they may be going back to soon.

"Somehow I knew you'd follow me in here." She said without looking.

"Well, I just wanted to make sure you were okay."

"I am. I just wanted to see it one last time. It really is so beautiful in all its simplicity. Just a ball, floating. The way it floats is just, well, wondrous."

Gary tried to play it cool and walked up to the glass. "Yes. And we're the only people in the world that ever got to see it like this."

Amber smiled a little bit. "I guess you didn't need me after all. Or anyone else for that matter. Who was it that said if you leave something alone long enough it will take care of itself?"

Gary pondered for a moment. "I wonder if you can look out these windows when you're going faster than the speed of light. I wonder what it would look like."

"We may find out yet."

Amber took a step back from the glass and cocked her head to one side. "Gary," she said, "I think we're getting closer."

Gary smiled a little. "I'm glad to hear you say that, maybe when we get back and things settled down..."

"Not that, you idiot." She said, rolling her eyes. "I think we're getting closer to the Earth. I think we're moving."

Gary wasn't sure whether to be embarrassed or concerned. He looked closely at the Earth and watched as a star faded behind it and the dark side started to become more visible. It was like their perspective was changing.

He looked at Amber. "I think you're right."

"What does that mean?"

"Not sure, but I'd better find out." Amber followed him out of the room.

He went to the men's hold first and sure enough, there was Matt and Melody, and it appeared that he was interrupting an argument.

Matt saw them first. "Hey Gary, Amber, what's up?" he said, welcoming the distraction.

"We're moving."

"It's a bit late, we have to get off the ship now."

"Not that, the ship is moving."

Matt and Melody exchanged a quick glance.

"I thought it was bad if we were moving. I thought if we moving it meant we're going to Mink."

"Well, yeah, that's what I thought."

Matt looked at Melody. "Go back to the hold and sit tight. Gary and I will go find Bob."

Gary said the same thing to Amber and the two men hurried out into the hall and nearly flattened Joel. "Oh, good…" was all he got out before they dragged him along down the long corridor.

As they passed the model's hold they ran into Parminder, Karen, and Becky coming out.

"Hey," said Karen, "We're worried about Terry, he's not answering our calls." She held up the remote that still had Terry's name written near one of the buttons.

"We don't have time for that right now, we're moving."

The girls exchanged glances and shrugged their shoulders. "Moving to where? Is your hold out of bacon or something?"

Before anyone could explain they saw Bob coming towards them with Joe and the three scientists behind him.

As he walked up Matt asked him, "Bob, are we moving? Are we heading to Mink?"

Bob stopped and took the alien equivalent of a sigh. "Yes and no."

Joe stepped up. "I was successfully able to remove the navigation module, the ship did not start the journey to Mink." He seemed almost proud of this fact.

"Yes." Said Bob. "But the next module wasn't the spin down module, it was the next step in the program."

"You see," said Joe, and even through the translator he sounded nervous, "the ship wasn't just programmed to go to Mink. It was also, um, meant to orbit Mink and take scans of the planet and land us in the most remote spot that could also support humans."

"What?" said many people together.

"This ship can land?" asked Gary.

Bob looked at him. "No. It cannot."

"Huh?"

Bob gathered his thoughts. "This is a deep space exploration and cargo ship with a faster than light drive. It was never meant to even enter a planet's atmosphere let alone land on one. We have no idea what's going to happen. I've never heard of a mother ship trying to land before. It just isn't done."

"Can't we stop?"

Joe waved his arms a little. "No, we are already moving. If we skip the next module and go into spin down the momentum will just send us hurtling into the Earth like a rock."

Matt wasn't sure what to ask next and all Gary could think of was, "Can't we take manual control of the ship?"

Bob's eyes bobbed a little bit. "This ship has a class N faster than light gravity well drive. You can't just take manual control of a class N faster than light gravity well drive, it would be like trying to drive a room full of gromulets into a basket with a stick. It just can't be done."

Joe stepped up. "Whoever programmed this ship knew it could land and you humans would still be alive. We think our best bet is to just let it do it. Let it find a place to land. If we don't then we may crash into a major city, or an ocean, or any number of things that would wipe out a great swath of life on your planet."

Bob raised his hands. "Don't worry. We have about four hours. We just need to cram everyone aboard the remaining freighters and saucers and they can hover in space until we land. Then, if the ship collapses under its own weight or something then at least everyone is safe. We are going to load up the disabled freighter with supplies just in case and set it adrift, if anything happens at least we can retrieve that and have something to live on for a while."

"Okay."

"Okay."

"Sounds like a plan."

The humans all stood there, nodding their heads.

"Bob," said Parminder.

It took him a moment to pick out who was speaking. "Yes?"

"What happened with Terry? I've been worried."

Bob's eyes lowered. He wished he could remember her name, he would have spoke it at this point. Instead he put his hand on her shoulder, a very intimate move for a Gorgon, and the two looked at each other.

"I'm so sorry, Terry and Kevin are, well, they are no more."

Parminder put her hands over her heart and her jaw fell. "What happened?" she managed to ask.

"I was told Kevin was so distraught that he took his own life, then Terry did as well. I guess he did love Kevin that much."

Her eyes filled with tears. "Couldn't anyone stop them?"

Bob put his hands together. "Who are we to say when one's life should end? Sometimes there is nothing we can do."

Karen looked at the scars on her arms, if only that were true.

She hugged Parminder and after a moment of crying into her shoulder she led her back to the hold, with Becky right behind.

Matt lowered his head. "Bob, shall we meet in the empty hold again?"

"No, we will have a service when this is all over, there is too much to do right now and all our lives are on the line."

Tatianna and the others headed back to their hold leaving the three men and two aliens alone in the hallway. Except for the absence of Kevin it was very much like their first meeting once again.

Bob turned towards Joe. "I've been doing some mental arithmetic, I don't think we can all fit on the ships that are left. I'll need some volunteers to stay on board. I will and we'll at least need an emergency crew and perhaps whoever is the expert on gravity wells, I'm not sure what will happen to it when we land."

Joe raised his eyes just a bit. "I'll stay, too."

Bob looked at the three men. "You had better go tell all the women that it will be a tight squeeze. No souvenirs I'm afraid."

The three men exchanged glances.

"Bob," Gary said, "We'll stay, too."

Bob looked at them. "No, it's too dangerous, we really have no idea what's going to…"

"Bob," this time it was Joel who interrupted. "On Earth we have saying, friends don't desert their friends in their hour of need."

Matt nodded. "You've done so much for us, and you're about to do so much more, if this ship crashes you won't be able to get home, that's going to be quite a sacrifice. We'll stand by you come hell or high water."

"You know," said Bob, lightly bumping his eyes together, "I think humans have a faulty survival instinct. I am surprised, and honored, by your sense of duty and friendship."

Joel smiled. "Well alrighty then. Let's land this Tub."

45

Karen led Parminder to the main table and they both sat down, Parminder still crying at the thought of losing her friend. On the other side of the table sat Cindi, pouring something from a box into a Coach bag.

"What's up?" she said looking up.

When Karen or Parminder didn't speak Becky said quietly, "Kevin and Terry killed themselves."

Cindi paused. "Terry was the one assigned to us, wasn't he? That's terrible, I liked him."

Karen was surprised to detect genuine emotion in Cindi's words.

Parminder and the rest waited until everyone was gathered around so they'd only have to say it one more time. A quiet fell over the group as they stared at the table.

Amanda was the one to break the silence. "So, what happens now?"

"We go home." Karen said quietly. "Not sure what's going on but this ship is going to land, somehow."

Amanda looked around at all the faces, deep in thought. "It's hard to imagine," she said, "Just a week ago we were all leading normal lives, now we're about to spring the biggest surprise ever on the whole world. Everyone's going to want a piece of us."

"At what cost?" Parminder was still sniffling, trying to control herself.

Karen thought about the night she pulled a razor sharp box cutter up her arm. She didn't want to die as much as she wanted someone to know how badly she wanted to die. But she also thought about how some cultures would die for honor and this must be the decision Kevin and Terry made. Well, Kevin at least.

Her thoughts were interrupted by Joel walking into the hold.

"Ladies," he said. "The time has come to go. There isn't much room on the ships that are left so there is no room for anything. A Gorgon will be here in about an hour to take you down to the hold and take you back to Earth." He paused and swallowed. "I don't know if what I did is a curse or a blessing. I'm sorry I put all of you through all of this but in the end I think it will work out better for all of you. Karen is right, I chose with my, um, dick, but I don't think I could have chosen better. For what it's worth, I learned a lot from you, and from Marisa, and Gary and Matt. I know this isn't the last time we'll be together, but thanks, for not killing me mostly." He smiled and looked around the room.

Karen was the first to hug him, and whisper in his ear, "I'm so sorry about Marissa." The rest followed, although some reluctantly, for a long group hug.

***

"What about a piece of the wall? It must be similar to the growing wires."

Gary wasn't sure what he just walked in on. The women were gathered around the big table at the front of the hold that was covered in pieces of alien technology.

"I've tried, you can't cut it or break it. I asked for a sample and was told it was just part of the ship, they don't have replacement parts for doors and walls."

"Hello." Gary said, interrupting. "What's going on?"

Tatianna looked up. "We are trying to see what we can carry with us. For all the technology around us, none seems to be very portable."

"Did you just ask for samples? This isn't Star Trek, you know. They have no qualms with sharing what they have."

"Oh, we were given samples of this biowire stuff and end point paint or whatever it is."

Gary leaned in. "I saw that. Were you able to make any sense of it?"

A few of the women looked down. Dr. Willhouse cleared her throat. "Well, um, we were able to make this." She held up a statue of Abraham Lincoln, which was the last thing Gary expected. It looked like it was carved out of wax. "It's not much, but it did it on its own, which is really fascinating."

"Okay." Gary nodded assuringly, although he wasn't sure who he was trying to assure and of what.

He looked around at the group, noticing Amber just sitting on a stool, just watching.

"A gorgon will be here in an hour." He said. "There isn't much room, so you can't take anything that won't, say, fit in your pocket or sit on your lap. From what I'm told. But I don't think you have to worry. I think you ten, above the others, will become the liaisons for the aliens back on Earth. This is really going to change things."

"Wait!" Said Dr. Collum. She tugged at Captain White's sleeve and hurried back into the maze of the hold.

Before long they returned with a box of wine glasses and a bottle of champaign. The glasses were handed out and Gary was given the bottle to uncork.

Smiling he said, "This is perfect, just perfect." In a few moments they all had a glass.

"To Group Two. I wanted help to get off this tub but instead found ten reasons to stay. May the ten of you help usher in a new age of mankind."

"Hear, hear!" Everyone clinked their glasses together which was followed by a few moans, coughs, and even a gag.

"This is the worst champaign I've ever tasted." Someone said.

"Now I know why I don't drink." Said another.

After a few moments Gary filled all the glasses again.

***

"I just don't know what our legacy will be." Isabel sat on a couch with her arms crossed. After Matt delivered the news he left with Melody leaving the rest of the women to ponder the future.

Isabel continued. "We all know we were picked so Melody wouldn't get jealous, we're not models, we're not scientist, we're just some broads who were trying to get by."

"That's not entirely fair." Kim said. "I've known Matt for years, he has a heart of gold, and if you think that he thinks any less of any of you then you're wrong."

"You can have a heart of gold and still do something wrong." This time it was Donna chiming in. "He may have been protecting Melody's feelings, sure, but at the cost of ours. How is all this going to look when the press starts getting all the stories?" She raised her eyebrows and did a poor impression of an anchorman. "And this just in, ten women were chosen for their beauty, ten were chosen for their brains, and a good seven others were picked based on being less attractive than a farmer's wife." She looked up at the low ceiling. "We really are the brawns, and when morning talk shows need an interview we are going to be the last in line."

Tracy shrugged her shoulders. "You know, I've given this a lot of thought. And in a way you are right, but in another way it just shows that anyone could have been picked to come up here. I'm going to use this opportunity to get in shape, to show the little chubby girl who's always picked last for gym teams that you can still do something with your life."

"Like be good at random chance?" Donna sat up straight. "Let's face it, we were the ones chosen last. I'm not saying anything bad about Melody, I'm sure she's a wonderful person, but we were all chosen based on being less than her. And again, not saying anything bad, but she's no super model, so Matt had to go

pretty far down on the totem pole to find us.
Yes, he's kind, he brought up a baby, he brought
up you," she gestured towards Kim, "but in his
attempts to spare her feelings, he made me, for
one, feel like crap. And yes, I'll jump at any
chance I get to be on Letterman or Ellen as one
of the first people to make contact with an alien
race, but in the back of my head I'll always
know why." She almost had tears in her eyes at
this point. "That will be a hard thing to
overcome."

Kim lowered her head. "I'm sorry. I
had no idea how, well, serious this all was. If he
were here now I know he'd feel terrible. Just
try to remember he was abducted, too, and had a
short time to figure out what to do."

Marie, who was flipping the lighter over
in her fingers wishing she had a cigarette stood
up. "Hey," she announced loudly. "Let's not
all turn into downers, remember it was one of us
who blew the lid off of this scam. Well, kind of.
And we are one of the first few people to
encounter an alien race. And if we're going to
be call the brawns, then I'm going to be damn
proud I'm a brawn and if we all stick together
we're going to be the best damn brawns in all of
history. Who's with me?"

"I am with you." Isabel stood up. "As long as we stay together we can take the world by storm." She held out her hand to Rachel. Very reluctantly she stood up.

"Yeah, okay."

After a few moments all were standing and hugging each other and wiping tears out of their eyes, until Kim tried to hug Donna.

Donna looked at her and raised an eyebrow.

"What? I'm a brawn, too."

"Ladies, what do we think?"

Tracy smiled. "Well, someone has to carry our baggage."

"Okay, then, you're officially a brawn. This is something no one can take away from us, ever."

The door opened right at that moment and Melody came in. Tears were running down her face and she could barely manage a glance at the other women.

"What's wrong?" asked Kim, going up and putting an arm around her shoulder.

"Matt's staying. This ship is going to crash into the Earth and Matt wants to stay on board. And he's making me leave. And...why are men so pigheaded?"

Isabel put her arm around Melody and together her and Kim walked her into the hold. "You're not alone, sweetie."

"Yeah," said Donna, "We all think men are pigheaded."

46

If Bob were a human with hair, he would have been pulling it out about now.

He looked around at all the activity in the saucer hold and barely any of it made sense. A young Gorgon pilot carrying a few satchels was running by and Bob had to reach out and grab him to get his attention.

"What on Gorgon is going on here? I thought I said no baggage."

The Gorgon who had no idea his translated name was Ted looked at Bob reluctantly.

"Well, a personal satchel does fit right under the seats so we just thought we could bring a few things."

"The personal generators and survival packs are under the seats." Bob said, as if this should be obvious.

Ted bobbed his eyes a bit. "Well, there is electricity all over the Earth, we didn't think we'd need them." He gestured towards a wall where hundreds of personal generators and survival packs were hastily stacked.

"But there are condensed nutrients in there as well, and tools…"

"Yes, well, we filled the disabled freighter with nutrients, it could last a year, plus what's on board Tub, plus humans have what's needed to make more."

Bob looked at the satchel Ted was carrying, just a few tassels hung out of it. "Are you bringing clothes?"

Ted waved his free hand. "Well, my moms knitted these, they have sentimental value."

Across the hold Bob spotted four Gorgons carrying a huge box into a freighter. "What is in that?"

Ted looked across. "Oh, one of the humans pointed out that if we do indeed land in a remote area and we can't get to the ship then they would need food as well. That is a box of what they call bacon."

Bob nodded. "Well, okay, I approve of that. Good thinking. But we can't take anything else…" He spotted another pile of equipment hastily stacked against another wall.

"Are those space suits? Did you remove all the space suits?"

"Well, not all of them. Some of the humans brought some clothes, and we added, um, well…"

"What? What did you add?"

"Squirt guns."

"What in the seven pillars is a squirt gun?"

Ted smiled and relaxed a little. "Oh, they're just the funnest things."

"All of this could have been left on board the Tub."

Ted fidgeted a bit. "Well, no one has ever landed a deep space freighter before…"

Bob knocked his eyes together. "Just please tell me that everyone who is supposed to get off this ship can get off."

"Oh, yes, quite. It won't be a problem. We'll hover for a bit then follow you down. One of the saucers will follow you down in case we lose tracking and to pass back news. The rest will stay out here until after the crash."

Bob squinted. "Land, we are going to land. You left room for the humans, right?"

"Oh, yes."

"Just make sure. Make sure everyone is off of this ship in an hour. And just where are the humans?"

Ted looked around. "There were many here a little bit ago. Don't worry, we'll get everyone on board."

Just a few yards away Tatianna and Nola Blanchard were staring at a tool cart that had been pushed out of the way.

"Tools! Of course! Maybe we can grab some of these."

Carl who was escorting some of the women looked down at the tool cart, which was just like the one he had set up for himself.

"Well," he said, "many of these are one of a kind and should stay here in the bay in case they are needed. If you really want a tool then you should just take some that we have several of."

Nola and Tatianna exchanged glances. "Sure, we'll take anything."

Carl looked over the tray and picked up two items and handed one each to the two women. "We have several of these, they are easily spared."

Tatianna looked over the object in her hand. "It's a screwdriver."

Carl nodded. "Yeah, we have dozens of those."

Nola held up hers so Tatianna could see the end. "Mine has five points."

"Yeah," said Carl. "There's kind of a funny curse associated with these. When you need a flat all you can find are stars, and when you need a star all you can find are flats."

"We know the feeling."

Tatianna smiled. "We'd be honored if you'd let us keep these."

Carl's reply was interrupted by another group of women entering the hold.

"Like you can't get those on Earth." Tracy was saying to Cindi, who had an arm full of silky dresses.

"And how many stores carry clothes that have actually been into outer space? Go ahead, name one. And these came from Paris."

"That's not the point, the point is we're supposed to be low on space, so essential items only. At least we can follow simple directions."

"Well, maybe one of you can stay behind and then we'd all have room for more..."

Before she could finish Tracy lunged at Cindi, giving her a push that sent her sprawling across the floor. Several women grabbed her and pulled her back but no one held Cindi who jumped up and dove back towards Tracy. Faster than the humans could react two Gorgons grabbed Cindi's arms and stopped her dead in her tracks.

Tatianna and Nola ran up between them, not sure what, if anything, they could do.

"Will you just please," said Tatianna in a strained voice, "just get to your ships? We are going home, and this is just about over. Could you act like humans for just a few more hours?"

Cindi jerked her arms free and smoothed out her dress. Still giving dagger eyes to Tracy she scooped up the dresses, turned her back and walked away with a few other models. Tracy also shook herself off and stood up tall.

"I'm sorry, but I really hate that woman."

Bob lowered his eyes and head for the nearest exit, behind him he could hear Tracy saying even louder, "Hate, hate that woman."

Down the hall he ran into Matt, Joel, and Gary who immediately asked what was to happen next.

"Just two things." Bob replied. "First we need to get to the centermost control room, and second, you need to explain to me why your females keep fighting each other. I mean, how does your race survive?" Without waiting for an answer he led the men down the hall.

**

Bob entered the control room and sat down next to Joe, who was already monitoring several systems. Three seats tailored made for humans extended from the back wall and this time each had two handles that extended from the seats to the head rests. When Joe had made these he figured the humans would need something to hold on to, just in case.

For a few moments all Bob did was look over the multicolored monitors that lined the control panel and the few big ones on the wall above it. He idly poked a few switches and moved some displays around before settling in on a configuration he was comfortable with.

"Let's see, where do we stand?"

Joe pointed at some alien language while the three men just looked over their shoulders, but the only thing that made sense to any of them was rapidly spinning Earth drawn in outline on one of the monitors.

"The damaged freighter is loaded and launched. There are two pilots on board and they said they might be able to land it in a pinch, but for now will just hold an orbit. Some ships are launching now and will just hold in the position we held until we land, then they'll follow us in and land around us."

"I want to make sure all the humans are on board. After the last ship launches I want a head count."

"Right. The gravity team are on board and have taken up in the control center just down the hall. They're not sure how the artificial gravity will react when we land, but they are ready for just about anything."

"You mean they can hit the off switch at any moment?"

"Basically, yes, that's all they can do."

"Who else will be on board?"

"There is a structural repair team of three. They are hanging out with the gravity guys. They seem to think as long as we don't hit too hard we should be okay, unless the gravity well or something does something unexpected, then we'll be crushed like seeds. We have just about completed the scanning orbit, any second now the program will decide where to land. It doesn't know that's not Mink, so it will still pick the most remote spot."

Gary nodded and used some of the trivia stored in his brain. "Tristan da Cunha. Most remote spot on earth. But it's an island."

Joe turned one of his eyes around. "We won't land on an island. Their plan was for you guys to breed and spread, that wouldn't happen on an island."

"Oh, yeah, then probably the Pacific Northwest."

Joel shook his head. "Amazon rain forest.   Right in the middle."

"Would it land us at a pole? Antarctica has nothing on it." Matt was drawing a blank as to where he thought the most remote area would be. "Middle of the Sahara desert, maybe?"

Again Joe disagreed. "There's nothing to live on at the poles. A desert? I'm not sure, it may consider that not enough to live on either."

Several red dots lit up on the map of the Earth and all five watched as they blinked out one by one until only one lone dot remained. It pulsed gently.

"There's the spot." Bob said.

"Oh, crap." Joel said.

Matt shook his head. "Well, that's the last place I wanted to go."

All Gary could muster was, "Huh."

Bob looked over his shoulder. "Do you men know that area?"

"Only in legend." Matt smiled.

Gary jumped in. "Well, no doubt it's isolated. Cold, brush, thick forest. Actually I'm not sure what's there, maybe tundra. It's a very paranoid government, though, I can see them being hard to deal with. I wouldn't be surprised if there were secret bases. Oh, and I think they did nuclear testing there."

"As large as this ship is," said Bob, "I doubt very much anything on Earth can detect it so we'd have to practically land on a secret base. We will be invisible to your radar, we don't emit any electromagnetic waves, and even if someone is looking right at us we'll appear to be no more than a meteor, which your Earth is bombarded with constantly. Plus the program will make us as stealthy as possible. I think for a while anyway we can evade whatever government is there."

Gary nodded. "We should inform the ladies. Do we have a way of sending them a message, all at once?"

Bob looked back at the controls. "I can inform the pilots of any ships that have humans on them, they can tell them. We should wait until they are all loaded, so we don't miss any. What shall we tell them?"

Gary pondered for a moment then said, "Just tell them Siberia. We'll be landing in sunny Siberia."

"Wait," said Matt, "Let's not tell them, let it just be a surprise."

Bob turned around to look at more displays. "As you wish."

***

Captain White stood hunched over in what could only be described as the cockpit of the saucer. She tried to make sense of the displays and was disappointed that there were no moving parts at all. No yokes or joysticks or throttles, just readouts and messages that they tapped on when they wanted something to happen.

"So, what do you do if you're in a storm, or something approaches you?"

The Gorgon known as Pete pointed to a display that had dots and alien captions on it. He was enjoying the attention as he explained how his little ship worked and his copilot who was still nervous around humans was happy to let Pete have it.

"Well, this monitors everything that can be a threat and routes accordingly. Or it can send out a gravity pulse and repel anything that is inconsequential, like small debris and such. As far as a storm, well, it would have to be pretty powerful to even effect us, maybe on a gas giant or something."

"You've flown into a gas giant?" Nola was behind Captain White and was just listening in up till now.

"Well, I haven't, but others have. I'm just saying that's the kind of wind and turbulence it would take to overpower the drive and hull. On a rocky planet, like Earth, you just don't see those kinds of forces. And these are the latest technology, I'm not even sure what some of this does." Pete poked a symbol and a loud unnerving clunk vibrated the craft. His eyes raised up as he quickly tapped the symbol again causing another, more soothing clunk. "Perhaps I should leave that one alone."

Captain White was still disappointed. "Do you ever fly manually? Or does the computer do every little thing?"

"Well," Pete said, "I don't see the need. We never really need to fly manually. If I tried to do all the computations the computer did in my own brain I'm sure we'd crash before I even got started. Maybe if we were travelling extremely, and I mean really extremely slow, in the open, with no obstacles, I could maybe do it. I know you fly jet propelled aircraft that can't leave the atmosphere with no computer or shielding and I think that's utterly terrifying. I wouldn't want to that at all."

"Oh, I must take you up sometime, it's the most fantastic thing in the world and I'm one of the few people on Earth who get to do it. To me this is like flying a house where all you have to do is put in an address and set the thermostat and sit back and have some tea."

Nola was still shaking from the clunks and was wondering why no one else was. She turned around to find her seat. "Best way to fly, at least for me."

"You know," said Pete, in a proud tone, "My great-grandmother was on the mission that first came to Earth. After it was discovered that there was advanced life here it was of great interest. Advance life has been exceedingly rare so far."

"Really?" said Captain White who was still staring at the control panel. She didn't want to seem rude but non-flight talk wasn't interesting to her at the moment, flying an alien space craft with advanced technologies was foremost on her mind.

"Yes. He used to tell me stories. Humans were popping up all over the Earth at that point and they tried to teach them metallurgy, disease control, navigation, math, things like that, but all the humans seemed to be interested in was stacking stones."

"Stacking stones?"

"Oh, yeah, great big huge piles of them. I took some pictures for him, they are still there."

"Wait." Captain White snapped back into the moment. "What big piles of stones?"

"Oh, they're all over. He said humans loved stacking them, the bigger the blocks the better."

Pete's copilot interrupted. "Incoming message, Pete. Bob wants to know exactly who is on board." He looked over his shoulder. "I'm sorry, but I don't know your names."

"Just tell them Evelyn White and Nola Blanchard is on board."

***

Bob was tapping at lists as symbols changed colors. "Okay, that's all the Gorgons but that's only 28 humans." His voice sounded almost in a panic. "I need a recount, there are only 28 humans on board the ships."

A voice answered from somewhere on the console. "Oh, Bob, we have that baby thing on board, too."

Bob lowered his eyes a bit. "Okay, that's 29. Don't ever do that to me again."

Joe tapped at some more screens. "Bob, we are changing direction, but the program doesn't show it. I think it's programmed to keep itself secret, even from the main controls. If I didn't have the external monitors on we'd never know we were landing."

"I really hate those bastards. If I ever get back to Gorgon I'll be ripping some eyes off, I can tell you that."

Suddenly the floor lurched up and Bob and Joe were pressed into their stools. The three men, who had been standing behind looking at the displays were knocked to the floor.

Gary could barely raise himself back up. "Holy hell, how fast are we going?"

Bob, who was also having to strain to hold himself up was frantically looking at the screens. "Oh, we are going exactly the same speed. For some reason the artificial gravity just doubled." He tapped a screen. "Lenny, what in hell just happened?"

A voice came through the translator. "The gravity just increased suddenly on its own but it's gearing back. Looks like it's adjusting to a hundred and twenty percent for some reason." There was a pause. "Jack said structural supports are popping up all over the ship as well. The program must be strengthening everything for entering the atmosphere."

"At least that's comforting." Bob muttered.

It took a few moments for the men to pull themselves up and sit heavily in their seats. They sat there breathing heavily.

"Hey guys," Joel said. "If anything happens I just want you to know I'm glad I met you. It's been great."

Matt and Gary nodded and muttered, "Yeah." All three men stared at the floor for a few moments while they felt the ship's gravity let up a little.

"Okay," said Matt, "Enough of the mushy stuff. How close are we, Bob?"

Bob was beginning to get nervous. "We are a few minutes from entering the atmosphere. The hull is designed to shield all kinds of radiation and small impacts but this will be a continuous friction. I hope those traitors know what they are doing. Those ignorant, stupid traitors."

"Our landing site is nearing termination. The daylight should shield our glow from entry, then nightfall will shield any search efforts, if there were any. I wonder if they planned it that way." He hung on for a few more moments. "Bob, even if we were to land fully intact I can't see how we can ever lift off again. We would need thrusters or something and there just aren't any big enough…"

"Joe," Bob interrupted. "One thing at a time. Let's just see what happens. Is the chase ship still there?"

"Yes."

All 5 beings held tight to their chairs. It was that moment where everything was out of everyone's hands and they all knew it. The men were pinned to their chairs which made the waves of vibrations even more apparent and unnerving. They watched as Bob and Joe lowered their eyes and mouths toward their bodies, almost as if they were making themselves into little balls with their feet curling up to hold themselves even tighter against their stools.

Still in orbit all the Gorgons and women were glued to monitors where the chase ship was broadcasting the landing for everyone to see. The ship started glowing against the white green blur of the land below it. A tiny yellow tail appeared behind it as the hull became white hot.

A voice came over an all ship broadcast, "We have lost contact with Bob."

In spite of all their differences and all the emotions that were being brandied about none of the women could stand the thought of their three comrades being inside that tiny glowing ball as it hurtled towards the ground. It seemed incredibly tiny and insignificant against the vastness of the Earth passing below it.

Suddenly, it was gone.

The broadcasted voice, which crackled with emotion, said simply, "Impact."

47

The vibrations grew stronger with each wave and over the speaker one of the other Gorgons was moaning with fear. Everyone gripped their seats and stared wide-eyed at nothing in particular.

Then, suddenly, everything was still. Absolutely still and quiet. Nobody moved or breathed.

A slow steady vibration started and Joe gathered himself together and tapped at his displays. He almost started laughing hysterically.

"We're down. We landed. The ship is almost on its side but it's rotating on one axis to right itself. Bob, it's over."

The eyestalks of each Gorgon started bobbing up and down like 4 weights on springs. The men, still slightly pinned by the increased gravity began to relax and carefully consider that everything was over.

"Well, that wasn't so…"

Suddenly a frantic voice came through the translator.

"Bob, we have to get off the ship." The voice screamed. "The drive is breaking lose, it's going to fall towards the gravity generators."

Bob could barely speak. "Where? How?"

The voice came back. "Head towards hanger four, it will be nearly ground level when the ship stops turning."

Bob and Joe hopped up and headed towards the door but stopped just outside.

"Gentlemen, we have to leave. Now!"

The three men were struggling with the increased gravity which caused the floor to feel like it was moving back and forth and lifting up at the same time.

"Easy for you to say," grunted Matt. "You have three legs."

The Gorgons reached out to help them and pulled them along the corridor.

The frantic voice came back over the translator. "Bob, brace yourself…"

Before it finished the ship lurched downwards and towards one side and all five were thrown against the wall.

Gary stood up and pulled Joel to his feet. "At least the ship stopped moving."

Trying to stand, Bob said, "We stopped moving moments ago, I think the gravity generator just went offline. Welcome back to Earth, this is your own gravity now." He seemed almost sad as saying it.

They ran into a small control room with windows overlooking an empty hanger. With a shock Joel recognized it as where Marisa lost her life. Bob pressed a few controls just before they crowded into the elevator and dropped down to floor level.

A few tool benches and scattered tools littered the wall the ship was leaning towards. The doors were already opening when they reached the far side and five other Gorgons were there waiting.

"Is everyone okay?" Bob asked as they reached the door.

"Yes," one said. "Well, one of us came uncoiled but I won't mention names."

Bob rolled his eyes as the bottom half the door finally reached the floor.

They all stood frozen as a cool breeze blew in their faces and they were presented with a forest that seemed oblivious to their arrival. Pines and birch trees swayed gently and birds could be heard chirping as if nothing happened. The sky was yellow and orange as the sun was near setting.

Looking down there were some crushed trunks and fresh earth which were the only signs that a gigantic space freighter had just plowed into the pristine wilderness.

As the Gorgons weren't running for their lives the men calmed down a little and took in the site before them.

"I can breathe." Gary said. "At least we aren't suffocating."

"No." said Bob quietly. "That was all a lie. For all of us."

Tub grumbled one last time and Lenny, a gravity engineer turned towards the rest and raised up a small personal pad and tapped at some screens. "I'm sorry Bob. The main drive crushed the gravity generators, and without those the bottom eight or so decks went with them. But it looks like everything is settled, we're safe now. No explosions, which is always good."

After a pause he added, "I'm sorry, Bob, but Tub, as we know it, is gone."

Bob's eyes lowered almost level with his body as did Joe's.

"I'm so sorry, Bob." Said Matt.

"There was nothing else we could do. At least we are down, and safe, and we can carry on."

Joel looked up and saw a flying saucer hovering at just treetop level. "That looks like a bad B movie. I can almost see wires holding it up."

One by one the Gorgons jumped down to the twisted trunks below and made their way onto the forest floor. Bob left last.

"Well, we need to coordinate the landings and figure out what to do next." He said. After a double nod of his eyes he jumped down after the others.

The three men looked down at the drop below them, which looked about forty feet down.

"Um, I don't think I can jump that far." Joel said.

"No way I'm trying it." Said Gary.

They stared at the ground for a few moments then Matt looked up at Gary.

"Are you reunited with your soul yet?"

Gary nodded and looked towards the distant hills. "You know, I think my soul and I are just beginning. It's good to be home. Kind of."

"Yeah, I think you're right."

"Is this really Siberia?" Joel asked. "I thought there'd be snow."

All three men smiled and watched the Gorgons walking through the trees which looked not unlike a herd of deer.

Bob looked up at the bulk of the ship, glowing orange in the setting sun looking like a giant black marble pressed into the earth. On the ground it looked incredibly, mind numbingly huge. Behind it the sky was growing dark and he wondered what the stars looked like from this planet. A few more flying saucers appeared looking tiny against the bulk of the ship.

He could see the three men still standing in the huge hanger door, looking out towards the sunset. They looked very alien yet very at home at the same time. There seemed to be a million thoughts going through his brain coil but only one seemed to matter.

Closing his eyes he turned around and walked towards the others.